CASABLANCA STORY

GLOBAL AFRICAN VOICES
Dominic Thomas, editor

CASABLANCA
STORY

IN KOLI JEAN BOFANE

Translated by BILL JOHNSTON

INDIANA UNIVERSITY PRESS

Originally published as *La Belle de Casa* in French © 2018 Actes Sud Published by special arrangement with Actes Sud in conjunction with their duly appointed agent 2 Seas Literary Agency.

This book is a publication of

Indiana University Press
Office of Scholarly Publishing
Herman B Wells Library 350
1320 East 10th Street
Bloomington, Indiana 47405 USA

iupress.org

English language © 2022 by Indiana University Press

Manufactured in the United States of America

First printing 2022

Library of Congress Cataloging-in-Publication Data

Names: Bofane, In Koli Jean, 1954- author. | Johnston, Bill, 1960- translator.
Title: Casablanca story / In Koli Jean Bofane ; translated by Bill Johnston.
Other titles: Belle de Casa. English | Global African voices.
Description: Bloomington, Indiana : Indiana University Press, 2022. | Series: Global African voices | Originally published as La Belle de Casa in French © 2018 Actes Sud.
Identifiers: LCCN 2021022447 (print) | LCCN 2021022448 (ebook) | ISBN 9780253058799 (paperback) | ISBN 9780253058805 (ebook)
Subjects: LCSH: Casablanca (Morocco)—Social conditions—Fiction. | LCGFT: Novels.
Classification: LCC PQ3989.3.B578 B4513 2022 (print) | LCC PQ3989.3.B578 (ebook) | DDC 843.92—dc23
LC record available at https://lccn.loc.gov/2021022447
LC ebook record available at https://lccn.loc.gov/2021022448

For my father, Isasi Iloluka, and
for my children, Véronique Inkoli,
Margaux Kabwanga, Johan, Carla, and Issa Isasi

CONTENTS

CASABLANCA STORY

1

SOLAR WINDS

THE MOMENT THE story came out, the cry went up all over the neighborhood of Derb Taliane: *"Ichrak metet!* Ichrak is dead!" Sese Tshimanga wanted to be the one to tell Mokhtar Daoudi.

Daoudi did not seem surprised to hear it.

"Follow me," he said.

Sese entered the inspector's office and closed the door behind him.

"Take a seat."

For twenty minutes now, the young Congolese had been cooling his heels on a bench, waiting for the inspector to appear.

"Yeah, yeah, he's on duty. He's out and about, but he'll be back," he'd been told from behind the counter by a ripped young detective dressed like a rapper, in a Raw Uncut T-shirt, a baseball cap, and a heavy chain whose links looked like they were studded with diamonds. Sitting with three uniformed cops, he was passing the night as best he could, playing dominos while waiting for a crime to deign to happen. No one had asked Sese what he wanted; he was known to be a personal acquaintance of the chief. Sese had bided his time, but the moment the inspector set foot in the station, he'd blurted out the news.

"How do you know about it?"

"I saw the body."

"Where?"

"Not far from her place. It's awful, Mokhtar."

Sinking into his chair, the inspector studied Sese's stunned expression. Daoudi's mind was racing. He stroked his short beard, which was intended to brighten up his large face, with its protruding nose. He shook his head, topped by salt-and-pepper curls.

"Poor woman. You're sure she's dead?"

"Sure as I see you in front of me."

"I believe you."

Mokhtar Daoudi hauled his imposing frame out of his chair and gave a sigh.

"Come on, you can show me. Choukri!"

"Yes sir, inspector!" answered the bodybuilder in a voice like a double bass. He said it the way you perform a hip-hop flow, eyes hidden beneath the peak of his cap.

"Mind the shop. I'm taking Sese; he needs to show me something."

The police-issue Dacia turned out of Rue Souss in the Cuba neighborhood and hung a left onto Avenue Tiznit. Inside the car, Daoudi and Sese were quiet, both thinking about the same thing. They passed the library and the museum of the Hassan II mosque and took another left onto Rue Zaïr, heading for Derb Taliane. The light from the streetlamps vied with a dim red sunlight bathing the city; dawn was breaking on questions that needed to be answered, if God would lend his help, of course.

When Daoudi pulled up on Rue du Poète Taha Adnan, gawkers had already gathered at the bottom of the stone steps down which Ichrak appeared to have fallen. Silence hung over the scene. There was whispering, but the atmosphere was one of reflection. Heads turned when Sese and the inspector closed the car doors.

"Out of the way!" Daoudi shouted, wanting to begin his investigation. "How am I supposed to find clues if you mess up my crime scene?"

The crowd parted, revealing the twisted body of the young woman. She no longer looked like Ichrak; there was a gash across her throat that had also cut open her black gandoura embroidered with gold thread.

"Don't just stand there; give me a hand," said the inspector to Sese. "Get these people out of the way."

"All right, move aside; there's nothing to see!" the young man ordered.

The onlookers offered a few protests for form's sake, but they complied, taking one or two steps back to make room for authority.

"Yes, send an ambulance," the authority was saying, his cell phone pressed to his ear. "And get a move on! Are you waiting for the whole neighborhood to be awake? You're right next door. OK."

Hanging up, he studied the ground around him as if he didn't know what to do next. He took a few photos with his smartphone, then knelt to look at the neck wound. Examining the cut without looking into the victim's eyes was far from easy. He shifted position. Bringing his knees together, he assumed the posture of one praying. He let out a long sigh, and his shoulders visibly sank. All those present saw clearly how it was the ambulance siren that finally pulled the inspector out of his daze.

"You understand that I have to lock you up."

"You can't be serious, Mokhtar!"

"Who was one of the first at the crime scene?"

"Me."

"When did you last see her alive?"

"Yesterday evening."

"There you are. Those are the rules. One of the last to see the victim alive, one of the first at the place of the crime. I have to, Sese; your profile is suspicious."

"But I have an alibi."

"What were you doing going to see her at daybreak?"

"We had an errand to run."

"Never mind that—we'll look into it. In the meantime, take it easy. Are you innocent, or aren't you? I'll lock you up. Then, if it wasn't you that killed her, I'll let you go. Besides, you're familiar with our cells, right?"

"Yes. But come on, Mokhtar! Be nice. If it was me, I wouldn't have come running to let you know. I tried to call you several times, but I couldn't get a hold of you, so I went all the way to the station in person."

"True. But I have to write a report, and taking someone into custody is good for my stats, see. It won't be more than forty-eight hours. You don't mind doing that for a friend, huh? I swear I'll bring you food made by my own wife. Choukri, my right-hand man, will personally deliver it to your cell. You know him, the guy that looks like Booba the singer. Wait and see; you'll have a ball."

The two men were in the car heading back to the station. They were both pensive. The ambulance had taken the body to the forensic institute morgue. Inspector Daoudi had climbed up the steps at the bottom of which Ichrak had been found; he'd combed the alley at the top in search of clues and had found and photographed traces of the victim's blood. He'd then come back down and asked the few residents who were around the usual questions. In fact, at this end of the street, there were only some small warehouses and a few hardware shops that would open later in the morning; otherwise, it was lined by tall blank walls, which explained why there were so few passersby at daybreak. The inspector had then made some notes, taken a few more pictures, and picked up some cigarette butts, which he slipped into a small plastic bag to legitimize his presence in front of the onlookers; then he left in the company of Sese Tshimanga. The first steps in the inquiry had been carried out zealously, officially, by the book.

The city was slowly stirring. The neighborhood merchants were setting up their stalls, voices were calling to one another, life was resuming its course. Derb Taliane, where the news of Ichrak's death was beginning to spread, was waking from a night that had been especially violent, to judge by the pool of blood drying at the foot of the steps on Rue du Poète Taha Adnan.

~

A pale hand bearing an indigo tattoo rested gently on the throat, concealing the dark laceration; the other, closed in a fist, was passing a wet cloth between Ichrak's heavy breasts. The water trickled toward the stomach and sides, then spilled onto the marble slab where the young woman's body lay. Old Zahira held herself straight. She wore a white gandoura; her head leaned to the side, her hair was loose. The neckline of her robe was awry, and the light from a high window shone on a bare shoulder, the skin wrinkled and marked with blue arabesques. She lifted her head with a groan.

"*Wili!* Calamity!" she said suddenly; her body folded in two and collapsed, arms stretched out, over the corpse of Ichrak, her only daughter.

A long, long sob burst forth, to the point of inhibiting her breathing. With her last strength, she filled her lungs so as to emit the wail that followed. It rose rapidly to her throat, against her will, using up all the air she had. It was unending. After a while, virtually emptied, she pulled herself together. With the back of her sleeve, she wiped her tears, which had smudged the kohl beneath her eyes. The one they called Al Majnouna—the Madwoman—was today condemned to the most merciless lucidity: Ichrak was truly dead. Compressing her lips in an attempt to suppress a prolonged moan, to lessen the feeling of suffocation, the old woman plunged the cloth into a plastic bucket and meticulously, with great tenderness, wiped this body that from now on would do no harm to anyone. Its mouth would remain shut forever; behind the closed eyelids, its gaze would no longer burn upon anyone. The stilled flesh was now as cold as the stone on which it had been laid, so it could be washed one final time, before being wrapped in a shroud and buried in the proper way.

~

A few months earlier, sitting on his bag at the side of the road, Sese had been unable to believe his eyes. Yet the billboard above him couldn't lie: five models dressed as Royal Air Maroc flight attendants, Hermès-style scarves around their necks, were aiming dazzling smiles at him, advertising special rates on all flights, with a text in Arabic and Berber entwined about them. There was no question about it: Sese was in Morocco. He'd noticed that the countryside didn't look like Normandy, even if he wasn't really up on French geography. Yet Normandy was where Farès Lefouili—if that was in fact his real name—had promised to drop him. The bastard. Sese could have wept with rage. He never should have trusted that nice-guy type. Sese hadn't seen it coming. They'd met in Dakar, at a table in Le Balajo, a small restaurant on Avenue Cheikh Anta Diop, not far from the port. An oversweet smile, honeyed voice, baby face, curly hair that was almost blond—all of that should have sounded warning bells: he was like a White. They were ruthless, those people, as he'd just been reminded. The guy said he was a sailor on a sardine boat that was leaving the next day.

Sese had just let on that he was aiming to get to Europe and that he'd fled Congo because of the political turmoil and the civil war.

"Everyone's fleeing these days, even the sardines."

At first the man had spoken to him of the tough economic times, caused by the industrial fishing vessels that sweep up everything.

"Those things are monsters! Japanese, Russian . . . What are the sardines supposed to do? So they got the heck away from Algeria! We thought we'd find some down this way, but all we caught were anchovies and jellyfish. When the pilchards saw our hungry mugs, they wriggled out of the nets and jumped back into the sea, I'm telling you. We're heading out tomorrow. We came all this way for nothing. Cheers."

The man raised his glass and drank. Sese followed suit.

"Do you know Deauville?" Farès asked after their third beer. "That's where we're heading tomorrow. Up there you've got all the fish you want. Scorpion fish, blue trout, mangosteens. It's in Normandy, in Francia."

"Damn! You don't say!" exclaimed Sese, already excited, his eyes glued to those of Farès.

Sese, who couldn't swim, had immediately thought that this was a way to get to Europe without drowning in a "Made in Senegal" pirogue, as he'd originally planned. So the two men cut a deal: a place in the hold of the ship for a fee of $500. After a further exchange of courtesies, they shook hands on $400. Farès had been classy about it and hadn't even insisted on a down payment.

"I swear on my mother, you'll love it up there!" he'd said, as if adding another clause to their contract. "My brother Yazid works at the Algerian embassy in Deauville; he can help you."

"What does he do at the embassy?" Sese asked.

"Everything!"

When Sese came aboard, the Algerian took his money—almost half of the dollars Sese had. The hiding place was a recess in the hold. There wasn't even room for Sese to stretch out fully. The voyage had seemed long to him, but in the end it wasn't long enough, because one night Farès opened the door and told him to take his bag. He hurried him down a deserted gangway toward a metal staircase. Sese was elated: he'd made it to Europe. For so long now, he'd been anticipating the moment when the cold that people talked about so much in Kinshasa would strike his face like a stamp in a passport, certifying his arrival in the Far North. But when a door opened on the night and the sea spray, Sese was more than surprised at the blast of heat that struck him. He didn't have time to think any further, because Farès led him running to a guardrail, on the other side of which a rope ladder dropped loosely toward the waves. Sese hesitated.

"What's this?"

"Climb down! There's no time for questions, the coast guard ships are close."

"But—"

Sese was cut off: Farès pushed him down into a rubber dinghy as deflated as a toy balloon after a party.

"Take that wooden thing over there. You know what you need to do now!" he shouted over the noise of the waves slapping against the boat.

Farès pulled on a cord and set the tiny dinghy free. It rocked alarmingly from side to side, like a kiddie pool.

"Hey!" squealed Sese.

A paddle lay on the canvas floor of the dinghy. Sese began to wield it desperately on either side, trying to hold his course. The moon faintly illuminated what he guessed must be an inlet. He managed to land on a pebble beach. A rocky path led up to what he hoped would be a road. He walked in darkness without knowing where he was going, up to the moment when the truth was revealed to him: he wasn't in Deauville; he wasn't in Normandy, as he'd been promised, but still in Africa—to be precise, in the Western Kingdom.

Since his arrival, he'd found his feet; he was able to express himself in a mixture of French, standard Arabic, and a little Darija, and he felt at home. But now, because of Mokhtar Daoudi, he'd found himself in jail without having done a thing, when all he'd wanted was to inform the appropriate authorities.

—

"Ah, Vié na ngai. Na barrer Ichrak? Ata yo moko. Moto na ngai. Ah, Great Man. Me, kill Ichrak? Can you imagine? She was my dear friend!"

Sese had uttered these words in Lingala slang, face lifted up, as if speaking to an especially influential divinity. Then he dropped into a sitting position on a cement slab furnished—if that was the right word—with a thin mattress that had been used for sleeping and a great many other things besides. His gaze moved around the cubbyhole they'd put him in, and he inwardly cursed Inspector Daoudi. Him, suspected of killing Ichrak? It was ridiculous! But that's what the inspector had claimed, booking sheet in hand.

Sese knew the man. Past fifty, Daoudi believed he had no time to lose and that his career deserved more than a small precinct in a crummy part of town. He would have preferred to work among the rich, not in a working-class neighborhood where people had nothing to offer him. At least, that's what he'd thought at first. Why bother arresting them if they didn't have the wherewithal to grease his palm? He'd moved heaven and earth to get himself a transfer. But recently things had changed, and a major upheaval was in the works around here. Like everyone else, he'd seen it coming; he heard talk of large-scale investments, and so his policing strategy had undergone an about-face. Arrests became the name of the game in Cuba and Derb Taliane.

He had to prove to his higher-ups that he was the man to watch over an area destined to accommodate multimillionaires. In Casablanca poverty was brazen; it didn't hide in the outskirts of the city but instead stared in the face of the wealth that flaunted itself with walls of concrete and glass designed by famous architects. To do the job properly, it would be necessary to expropriate and demolish the last hovels that devalued their surroundings, but the occupants had decided that their opinion mattered. They'd leave, but not without acquiring a little of the plenty being paraded before them. And so, quite naturally, they dug in their heels and resorted to extortion. The government had doubtless made a mistake in offering a sum of money for each expropriated family and relocation outside the city. Once this became known, the residents encouraged all the uncles, aunts, cousins, nephews, and nieces they could to move in from the country, so they could all benefit from the promised gold mine. Inevitably, the budget for the operation skyrocketed. On top of that, word got about that those who'd quickly accepted the offer had not found their new accommodations any better; on the contrary, those thoroughgoing city dwellers had been moved to a landscape that meant nothing to them. Things were at an impasse. The people and the state were eyeing each other, waiting for a solution to emerge, but alas, pride and a spirit of resistance were the specialty of Derb Taliane— they formed part of its letters of nobility; they were built into the DNA of all who were born there. Nothing could be done about it. It was the same in the Cuba neighborhood. Despite all this, Inspector Daoudi did not despair; all these people were bound to leave sooner or later. He thought ahead, even, and made up his mind to boost his stats. When crime rates looked like they were about to drop, arbitrary arrests multiplied for the smallest reasons. He'd promised himself he'd become the best-performing cop in the country, no less.

The next day, the papers would say that a woman had been found dead and that Inspector Daoudi had rapidly begun an investigation and made an arrest. In forty-eight hours, Sese knew, he'd be out again, after having bolstered the detective's score sheet for a moment. But forty-eight hours was time and money lost, thought Sese. As it was, things hadn't been going that well. Before he met Ichrak, his turnover had been in decline. The charm and sincerity he displayed with his big smile on the computer screens of European women were clearly insufficient: the Western Union transfers were barely trickling in; he was having trouble making ends meet.

The day he'd met Ichrak, it had been as oppressively hot as it was at present in his cell. The air blowing from the desert not only heralded sandstorms; it could also be bringing bad luck. Like now, thought Sese. That memorable day, he'd been so sick of it all that he'd decided to change his occupation. Sese was what's known as a *brouteur*, a sort of African cyber-seducer. One of those guys, often very young, who maintain a retinue of dozens—sometimes even hundreds—of women in love with them. These men are workaholic pickup artists trying to wrangle money from the women by playing on stereotypes of poverty-stricken Africa and the eternal guilt of a slave-owning, colonialist Europe in search of redemption. With this intense psychological strategy, the brouteurs made hundreds of euros a month, tethered to their keyboards, their screens, and their lies. Except that the virtual rendezvous were no longer such a profitable niche. The competition was getting tougher, and the various sites waged merciless war in their listings. So Sese had decided to switch to bank fraud—as a *shayeur*, or fly-by-night salesman, he'd already had some practice at this. Picking up young or older white women looking for love was right up his alley; it could even be regarded as a public service. Sese enjoyed uttering phrases that melted the hearts and the credit cards of his prey. "Listen me, you are only one make my heart beat so hard, I swear you!" he could say suavely in a Kinshasa accent. When the maiden laughed, he knew how to press his case and pursue the seduction. He was a sentimental guy, was Sese; emptying the bank accounts of suckers contacted by email was tiresome work, and it did a lot of harm to the victim, who was perhaps a little too keen, but innocent all the same.

It was out of desperation, then, that he'd wanted to apprentice in fraud with Dramé, a Senegalese hustler, but the guy didn't show that day.

"Fuck it!"

Returning home from his failed rendezvous, he'd had to run to catch his bus, panting in exasperation.

"I haven't got all day," the driver grumbled, his hand on the button that would close the door.

Sese didn't even respond. He bought a ticket and wove his way down the aisle looking for a free seat.

"Dramé's beginning to act the wise guy . . . I need training, me! I call him, he never answers, and when he does pick up, he makes a bogus appointment: 'Come to Place des Nations-Unies; we'll get a bite to eat.' Then he makes me wait like an idiot!" Sese found a spot next to a woman who seemed absorbed in the passing scenery. He brooded on his frustrations. His affairs were not going the way he would have wanted. He was wondering if his virtual sex appeal had dried up. Those damn women must have been spreading the word on some forum, saying that Koffi the Big Ngando—that was his online name, Big Crocodile—was nothing but a cheap swindler. He should look into it.

He was deep in his thoughts when there was a nastier-than-usual bend in the road, and he felt his pelvis sliding to the left. He had to hold on to the seat in front of him. At that moment an electric sensation originating at his right hip rippled through his entire body: driven by centrifugal force and the universal laws of gravitation, a firm, curvaceous flesh, endowed in addition with diabolical suppleness, had pressed against his own flesh and had muddled his spatiotemporal awareness for a good three or four seconds. The feeling gradually ebbed as Sese became aware that it was the hip and thigh of his neighbor that had been responsible for this inner turbulence. After the shock, a sweet warmth overcame Sese, and his mind left terrestrial reality behind for an indeterminate length of time. At that point, a low voice came from the woman's lips, whispering words in an emphatic, finely chiseled flow, with a rhythm that undulated like dunes in the desert standing out against the sky: *Of infinite length, the night will not offer me any rest, relieve me of any weight. Quite the opposite—it will give me ever greater clarity, and I shall see, as I have never before been given to see, to what point my presence here is in fact unknown, my needs unmet, my requests ignored; to what extent too, in this house all is conflict, struggle, and failure.* Wearing earphones, the young woman was reciting a text that caressed Sese's ears. The soft hiss of the bus's tires against the asphalt resonated in his head like a steady accompaniment. He closed his eyes, and the light, which had a slightly stroboscopic quality from the passing cityscape, intensified his flight of fancy. The thigh had not moved; on the contrary, its pressure had increased. A sweet tranquility swept over Sese Tshimanga. He wanted to yield to it, but he felt an erection twitching into existence, and that helped him collect his thoughts. Not wishing to become distracted and ill-mannered, he restrained himself and mastered the beating of his heart. The psalm-like chant poured irregularly, like a stream of honey, from the young woman's throat. Sese, eyes closed, was far away, while everyone else in the bus remained deep in the twists and turns of their own thoughts . . . *His head resting on my lap, I continue gently to stroke his face, his neck, his arm. I speak to him of the weather outside. It's sunny, I repeat, it's sunny, despite the rainwater dripping from the metal gutters, despite the absence of exterior light, despite the chill in the house. And without making any sound, I get up . . .* The bus rode on like a flying carpet. In Sese's head, at least, there was no doubt as to the marvel he was experiencing.

"Excuse me!"

Sese looked up and stared uncomprehendingly at the young woman standing over him. He jumped to his feet and let her pass. He must have dozed off. This was her stop. Looking out the window, he realized it was his too. As he got off the bus, the woman set off immediately down Avenue Tiznit, carrying a cardboard box under her arm. He followed her. In the bus, Sese had only seen her in profile. He'd caught a brief glimpse of her face when she'd risen to get off, but here he had before his eyes the outline that could be made out undulating beneath her full-length robe, which bore a leafy pattern in red, yellow, and green against a dark turquoise background. As she walked, at times the rhinestones adorning her sandals could be seen. Shoulders pulled back, she was like a sculpture, and the vigor of her body could be sensed from the movements of the fabric, whose resistance was most sorely tested at the level of her hips. Sese watched the play of the leg muscles as they pulled the buttocks taut. The hang of the garment was intended to hide this subtle mechanism, but Sese's eyes and his other senses once again found themselves troubled by the fluidity, the power, and the emotional force generated by the panther-like walk of the bus rider.

"Mademoiselle!"

"What do you want, kid?" she asked, barely turning her head.

"'*Of infinite length, the night will not offer me any rest, relieve me of any weight. Quite the opposite, it will give me ever greater clarity and I shall see, as I have never before been given to see . . .*' You could have kept repeating that sentence for a thousand and one nights; I wouldn't have said a word because you'd be giving me ever greater clarity."

"What is this? Are you spying on me?" the woman said with a scornful look.

"Don't be mad, my sister; I'm Sese."

"I'm not your sister."

"Mademoiselle, then?"

"Best not to talk at all. Look at yourself. And you're trying to pick people up? Buzz off!"

She quickened her pace and ignored him, looking straight ahead as she walked on. Sese caught up with her.

"Sister, I'm a poet too. Listen, this is a Cameroonian poem."

Keeping time with his right hand, he recited in super-precise rhythm:

Hey, my friend, see, you're not talking to me?
I say, come share a njoka with me and you put on airs?
I wanda about you, eh.
My friend, what's going on?
If you didn't want njoka,
Molla, you shoulda stayed home!
Stick to it, stick to it, baby.
Stick to it, stick to it, stick to it, baby.

"That's what you're doing? And you have the nerve to say it!" she exclaimed, one eyebrow raised. "You're nuts!"

"I'm just trying, sister; don't hold it against me."

The young woman stopped and studied Sese the way you'd examine an extraterrestrial whose dimensions went far beyond what you'd imagined. Then she burst into peals of crystalline laughter that to Sese's ears was like a melody from the heavens. Her face was already of an incomparable beauty, but when she laughed, her perfect features seemed suddenly illuminated as if by a spotlight, the way only the best movie directors know how. She was as tall as a daughter of the Kasaï region of Congo, and her hair, gathered in a bun, increased her height even more. A broad lock of hair lay across her forehead, and her almond-shaped eyes seemed to be holding back a lake at the rim of her lower lashes. A soft fold of skin hemmed them, no doubt restraining the excess of emotion that her gaze did not dare to reveal. That gaze was intensified by full, clearly defined eyebrows and long lashes. Her nose was straight. Her lips, fleshy as petals, had the color of glistening pomegranate, while her skin was copper hued. In the heat and the sunlight that burned everything around, a sublime vision had materialized before the young Congolese. He forgot about the tidal wave that had crashed against his right thigh; he could feel only his heart melting as swiftly as an ice floe filmed in time lapse. Ichrak was extraordinarily beautiful.

"You're crazy, kid," she said, breathing regularly again. "Make yourself useful; carry this."

She handed him the box that was under her arm.

"What's your name?"

"Ichrak. You're Sese, is that it? Where does that name come from?"

"Take note! It's a great name. I'm from the Congo. The Democratic Republic. The big one. Zaire, you know."

"What are you doing in Morocco? You're trying to cross, is that it? Into Spain?"

"I didn't plan to be here. You can't trust anyone in this world, sister. A crook left me here when he'd promised to take me to Normandy. I was supposed to get off in Deauville, then go to Paris on the TGV, direct. 'You know Deauville?' he kept asking me. The louse. I wanted to see Belgium, London, Paree. Not Morocco! I was on a boat; then I found myself here."

"You're not happy to be here?"

"Sure, but you have to understand: I thought I'd left Africa; I wasn't intending to end up back here. Especially against my will. But I'm adapting; I have plans. It's not bad here."

"So what are you doing in the meantime?"

"I'm a poet, I told you. I really liked the things you were saying before. A poet is sensitive to words."

"You can't live on words. I asked you what you do."

"I'm in business," said Sese evasively.

"What business?"

"I talk with people on the internet, and they send me money."

"You talk with women, is that it? Tell me the truth."

"I'm not doing anything wrong, sister. They need me over there. In Europe, men and women don't live together so much anymore, you know. It's all modern there. A lot of men live as couples together, so I've heard. So what are the women to do? Luckily I'm there for them. In the evening, after work and all that, when they need a bit of masculine company, they only have to turn on their computer, and there I am."

"And talking with you helps them in some way? All you do is tell them nonsense."

"Me, I'm just there to warm them up. After that, they only need to finish the job. There, in White countries, they've got objects they call sex toys. Apparently those things are stronger than their men. More effective. They work on batteries."

"I don't want to hear any more. It's disgusting, that business of yours."

"I've also heard that over there they think African men are super-powerful. So all the woman has to do is look at me on the screen and talk to me, and she wants it. That's why they give me money."

"Doesn't that make you a bit of a con man?"

"Not at all. They fantasize about my face, my voice. You don't expect me to give them all that for nothing?"

"Give them what? Have you seen yourself?"

Sese looked down at what he was wearing. In his Barcelona soccer shirt with the Qatar Airways logo, his jeans, and his red and blue Nikes, he looked pretty good, he thought. With that and his angelic mug with its short dreads, they had nothing to complain about.

"You give nothing, and you charge money for it? I wouldn't mind being in your shoes."

"It's easy, sister. You have to understand that it's all virtual. I was listening to the things you were saying before. I swear, if I could talk like you, I'd be raking it in hand over fist. We could go into business together. You'd be my communications consultant. In exchange for that, I'll train you, and you'll make yourself some dough."

"All you need to do is read some books, and you'll know as much about it as I do."

"Read novels? Me and literature, you know . . . I don't have the patience. I'm a businessman, a man of action. All I'm lacking is a dependable partner. Where do you live?"

"Derb Taliane. Why?"

"I'm nearby, in Cuba. You could come over to my place; we can run a trial. People need words like the ones you were saying. With that, sister, they'd be dropping like flies; I know it."

"Your place? You think I'm going to go just like that, with someone I don't even know? Who do you take me for?"

"Easy now, I was just talking. Trying to explain things to you. With the language I heard, you could make money easily, but for that you need a network."

Sese looked left and right, as if to ensure no one was listening, and said confidentially:

"I've got one. It's solid. To get the Western Union rolling in, you need to have a conversation, but at a certain point yacking doesn't cut it. Women need poetry; men need to see. We'll be there, side by side."

"Are you putting me on?"

"Not at all. Listen . . ."

Sese put the cardboard box on the ground to better convince his interlocutor.

"I've got all these women in my computer, but recently you'd think they'd been tipping each other off. When I press them for money, they block me without warning. I ought to add a box that they click on to say they accept my conditions before they can talk to me. Do you reckon my language has gotten limited?"

In fact, the young woman had thought so from the moment Sese had started reciting his crummy little "Stick to It" poem. On the other hand, he was right: women needed poetry.

"I'm not interested."

"If you start tossing out words like the ones you were saying, anyone'd be hooked; I'm certain of it. And I know how to make them pay. Frustrated people will always have need of us."

"Also, you don't even respect them, those clients of yours. You should be ashamed. I'm this way," Ichrak said, pointing down an alleyway that plunged into a kind of multicolored labyrinth of old houses whose walls and woodwork bore the patina of time. "This is where we part. I'll take my box."

"Hang on! Give me your number at least."

She took a cell phone from her leather handbag, pressed some buttons, and showed him a number on the screen.

"Here."

"Got it!" He tapped it in. "Tell me your name again."

"Ichrak."

"Whoa! That's complicated. I'm Sese. I'm calling you; don't pick up—that way you'll have my number too. Don't forget. If you hear, 'This is Sese!'—it's me. All right, sister. To be continued . . ."

The young woman walked off. Sese didn't leave right away. He lingered for a while, playing at making himself dizzy merely by keeping his eyes riveted on the powerful centerline of Ichrak's body as it shifted from one hip to the other. Holding his breath, he wondered how such a slim figure could coordinate those forms with such suppleness while making them describe their measured ellipses in space. It was only when he was on the point of collapse that he turned and walked away, his senses even more disturbed than they'd been at the moment the two of them met.

~

"Ah, Vié! Tala kaka! Ah, Great Man! Really!"

Still squatting in his cell, face and palms turned upward, Sese was once again taking the late President Mobutu as witness. The Great Man had died when Sese was still a child, but Sese considered him his mentor, his master in thinking, his source of enlightenment; at times of need like the present moment, he called upon him. Had he not been given the epithet of Guide? Sese, then, had taken him as his own adviser. When he had some question in his life, it was to Mobutu that he turned to resolve it. When adversity loomed, the Marshal was the shot of courage he needed. When Sese was feeling lonely and overcome by nostalgia, Mo Prezo was there to comfort him. To the younger man, he was like a superhero, because after all, this leader, born Joseph-Désiré Mobutu, had had to change his name to Mobutu Sese Seko Kuku Ngbendu Wa Za Banga—because no one is born with the name of Superman, the Hulk, Catwoman, or Spider-Man. For a time, you can accept being called Clark Kent in New York, Selina Kyle in Gotham, or Joseph-Désiré in Kinshasa, but at a certain moment you have a mission to carry out. That was indeed the duty felt by those in the personal pantheon of Sese Seko Tshimanga—for such was Sese's true patronymic.

Sese's worship of Mobutu came from long ago—from his father, to be precise. The latter was still in Mbuji-Mayi in eastern

Kasaï when the strongman came to power and eased restrictions on diamond mining. A teenager at the time, Sese's father, like most of the inhabitants of the region, had gotten it into his head to become what was called a "diamondist," so he could be rolling in dough, like the CEO of the Bakwanga Mining Company. It was at this time that the young Mwamba Tshimanga made his first dollars. He showed off a Newman denim outfit imported by a Lebanese and bought for an exorbitant sum, washed his moped in champagne while everyone watched, and laid all the chicks that not long before would not have given him the time of day. After that, his admiration for the Founder never wavered: his appeal for "National Authenticity"; the introduction of a new currency, the zaire, worth two dollars; the Zairianization of all foreign assets; and, of course, the move that the young Mobutist found most stylish of all—organizing the match of the century, Ali vs. Foreman, in Kinshasa. He adopted Mobutan sayings that became his life philosophy. These included "Corruption is a foreign import!" "Zairians don't steal; they merely relocate things"; and "High up in the air, the eagle does not fear the spit of the toad." All this combined to magnify the hero of the Battle of Kamanyola in Mwamba Tshimanga's imagination, and it was with such precepts that he achieved his rise through the ranks of the Kinshasa civil service within MOPAP, the regime's propaganda wing, which he had joined with his wife, a former classmate.

On April 24, 1990, there was a great upheaval in the life of Mwamba Tshimanga. On that mournful day, after locking down the entire republic, Mobutu appeared on television in his marshal's uniform, scepter in hand and teary-eyed, to declare before a full chamber, in front of the whole world, that he was opening the country up to democracy, to a multiparty system—and so on and so forth—and that he was stepping down as president of the state party. In other words, since in theory the president of the MPR party was president of the republic, in making this announcement, Mobutu was de facto giving up the position of president of the Republic of Zaire. The shock experienced by Tshimanga that day was passed on to his wife, who was over eight months pregnant at the time. Her contractions began immediately, and the child entered the world around three thirty in the afternoon. The young father, in despair, knowing he would be unable to bear the absence of the dictator, filled the yawning void by naming his son Sese Seko, like Mobutu Sese Seko Kuku Ngbendu Wa Za Banga. "No one will ever be as great as Mobutu, and my son will be there to remind future generations of Zairians of the times when providence was on our side," he declared solemnly to the mother and the two midwives present. "The operation of the mines will no longer be as joyful as in the days when every yard along the banks of the Lubilanji was occupied by a family, a secretary, a schoolboy, a civil servant, just after work, just before the time for an aperitif. Without him, hyenas and jackals will show their snouts," he predicted too. "Democracy!" Mwamba Tshimanga had long loathed that word. It was also true that around seven that evening Mobutu, smiling and relaxed, no longer in his marshal's uniform, his leopard-skin toque once again on his head, performed an about-face, live in front of the cameras of French TV, saying in surprise: "Me, no longer president? I said that? Really?" It did nothing but magnify the man even more in Tshimanga's eyes. A true head of state has to be capable of such a reversal—otherwise, how could he take part in the community of nations? Immersed in Mobutism since his earliest childhood, Sese carried his name with extreme pride. He would not have changed it for anything in the world.

"Vié, na regretter mabe—I really regret it, Great Man. If I'd stuck to your ideals and been cautious with Ichrak, I wouldn't have ended up here."

Because after all, Sese reasoned, Mobutu had forbidden men to look at a particular point of female anatomy, banning the wearing of pants in favor of the *pagne*, which was supposed to be more becoming in covering up the charms of African women. At that time, the president was concerned for both feminine and masculine sexes, wanting to protect the former from lustful glances, which were in total contradiction with the values of the republic. Sese had looked at Ichrak too much; because of that, he couldn't help striking up a conversation with her, getting to know her, and now he felt lost without her. In his mind he could still hear her laugh and see the sparkle in her eyes when they briefly met his. Sese lay on his back and went through his memories. With nothing but a couple of days of police custody ahead of him, he had the time. It was nothing, he told himself; he'd been through ups and downs before, after leaving Congo. During all this time, lying on his mattress or pacing his cell, Sese had been weeping for the woman who was his *pire moto na ye*—his own pure person, his closest friend—in this country. He wept for her till he was exhausted, and he didn't even notice that Daoudi's promise to bring him meals cooked by the inspector's wife had not been kept. From the flood of tears he'd shed, at one point he had the feeling that his body, which had broken into pieces several times before, was now as cracked as a land that had not seen rain in the longest time, and whose soil there was no hope, ever, of bringing back to life.

2

GEOTHERMAL POWER

FOR THOUSANDS OF YEARS, the Chergui wind had been descending upon the land, and the people had been putting up with it. Recently, though, the wind had been losing its supremacy over the regions it once traversed. Made strong by the depletion of protective ozone, Climate Change could now openly show its desire to seize power across the globe by any means necessary. One of its battles was currently being waged above Addar Al Baidaa', which some call Casablanca: Climate Change had made use of Chergui to master the city and its inhabitants while giving Tangiers and Essaouira a respite. Its principal ally, the Gulf Stream, had since time immemorial been attempting to enwrap the whole earth. All Chergui aspired to do was to pass over the Mediterranean via Gibraltar and the Balearic Islands, to press on toward Provence, Sicily, and Southern Italy, and to accomplish its appointed destiny by becoming the Sirocco in those regions.

This time, however, air turbulence had gotten in its way and forced it to turn back upon itself over the city, like in a turbine, searching for a way out. During this process it stockpiled heat—along with elementary particles no doubt—and in such a way, it was profoundly disturbing the souls that it governed. Chergui was customarily carried by winds from Arabia to the east and southerly winds that come from the vast Sahara. At a certain point in its trajectory, it was supposed to cross paths with the northeast trades, which would have helped it to cool down, but this didn't happen as planned. The Gulf Stream, with the support of Climate Change and global warming, had decided to go to work in the regions influenced by the Azores High, interrupting its route at the Canary Current and causing an extreme rise of energy in the very heart of Chergui. The latter, then, was sorely testing the nervous systems of humans and all that was closely connected to them, including their souls and their most deeply hidden emotions.

~

Inspector Daoudi hung up, put his phone back in his pocket, and waited, sighing as he thought about his work, which didn't let up. Even when he was off duty, he wasn't, especially when a body was discovered. Honest people would head home, whereas his job required him to keep different company, and it was during the extra hours, not prescribed by any verse in the Koran, that guys like Nordine Guerrouj moved about. The inspector couldn't do a thing about it; he wouldn't be relaxing any time soon.

A few minutes before, he'd parked his Dacia by the medina, on Avenue des Forces Armées Royales, in front of a bar where an unlighted sign was redeemed by another absurd one announcing in flashing red that it was OPEN. Soon, a man opened the passenger side door. In his early forties, good-looking despite the scar on his cheek, with wavy hair combed back, he was wearing jeans and a slim-fit blue shirt with a small white motif. On his feet he had stylish Armani tennis shoes, also blue. He sat down in the passenger seat and said, "How did you get this number? I've only had it for a couple of weeks."

"You think I've been asleep since then? I'm a cop, and I'm here as a cop."

"What is it, inspector? It's usually my cousin that you talk to. It's not good to be seen together, you and me. Not good at all. Plus, you went and parked right in front of my bar. What if someone spots us?"

"If you don't want to be seen with me every day from now on, tell me one thing: Where were you the evening before last?"

Nordine Guerrouj was silent for a few seconds. "What time the evening before last? What's this about, inspector? I was sitting quietly at my place."

"We'll look into it, Nordine."

"Why are you asking?"

"You know Ichrak?"

Of course he knew Ichrak. Alarm bells went off in his head at the young woman's name. Daoudi went on: "You know what happened to her?"

"Come on, inspector, you're not gonna pin that one on me! She's dead. So? That bitch pissed off a ton of people."

It was true that Ichrak had been a thorn in Nordine Guerrouj's side. He'd tried for a long time to get his hands on her, but despite his insistence and his threats, she'd always resisted, sending him back to his whores. He'd even decided to ignore her when she passed by, unable to bear her gaze as she scornfully looked him up and down. She was by far his biggest turn-on, but she wasn't like certain others who'd made the mistake of falling in love with him and who figured that, after all, with Nordine it was well worth sacrificing a part of themselves that could be converted into cash. He didn't know exactly how Ichrak made her living. For a time, he'd thought that she was simply discreet about her clients, but he was mistaken; she kept her body for herself. So what difference did her death make to him? She'd been a sort of challenge to his personality.

"Did I say you were the one that killed her?"

"No, inspector, you're not saying anything. But if you think I had anything to do with that business, you're mistaken."

"But you know things."

"Me, know things? I swear on my mother, I don't know anything!" He held his hand open in a gesture of complete innocence.

"Take it easy. You know everything that happens in the neighborhood. Like me. I know for instance that you've started warehousing merchandise somewhere in Derb Houmane. You see what I'm getting at?" Leaving Nordine and his scar a moment to turn pale, Daoudi added, "You can help me, like I'm helping you right now. Have my men been turning up here, then at your place, in front of your wife and children, arresting you? No, because I understand you."

Nordine studied the other man's face to see if he was joking. He started thinking real fast. He mustn't panic. If the cop had wanted to arrest him, he'd have called him in to the station instead of coming over in his crappy car.

"We understand each other, you and me," Daoudi repeated. "Do the math about the merchandise. We'll meet again tomorrow and talk some more."

"No problem, inspector."

Nordine was relieved for now. He'd thought he had a safe hiding place. His hand on the door handle, he went on: "We'll see each other tomorrow for sure. Like you say, you and me, we understand each other."

"Don't be too sure, Nordine," Daoudi said.

"You've got my number."

The hoodlum got out of the car, somewhat reassured but still not completely set at ease. This Inspector Daoudi was a real motherfucker. Standing on the sidewalk, Nordine watched the detective's car pull away, then, after a moment, hang a U-turn and head toward Place des Nations Unies. Nordine spat on the ground to summon all kinds of evil fates for him and cursed Daoudi as he walked away: "Rot in hell!"

The detective didn't go quite so far—no doubt it wasn't the right moment. Stopped at a red light, he had to exercise his patience because despite the hour, traffic was pouring in from the right. To the left, in front of the main gateway of the medina, the stallholders were still far from calling it a day. On the Esplanade des Nations Unies, street musicians with portable sound systems, each more powerful than the next, had divided up the space as they performed traditional music, rock, R&B, or Cabrel, with varying degrees of talent, for their admirers. Itinerant salespeople hawked their wares among the onlookers and the families out taking a stroll and enjoying the life of the city, amid the noise of cars brightening the night with their strings of lights, white in front, red behind.

When the light turned green, Daoudi shifted into first gear and set off slowly. For a while he drifted left toward Boulevard Félix Houphouët-Boigny. Darkness had settled in and was playing its part in enlivening the mood. The passersby were just as numerous at the stalls selling souvenirs in iron, pewter, leather, wood—objects that had been hollowed out, chased, engraved, polished, planed, forged, painted, assembled using techniques that had come from ancient times. The sky had donned its cobalt-blue cloak, dotted with bright microscopic grains of sand. Chergui was keeping up constant pressure on the environment, on bodies, and on souls. In the way it shook the crowns of the palm trees, it seemed to be expressing its power through an allegory of the wild hair of madwomen thrashing in the grip of merciless demons. There'd been a brief respite since the morning Ichrak's body had been found, as if, after passing through the neighborhood, it had been exhausted by the task of having a young woman murdered in the middle of the night.

Daoudi was crawling along, cursing himself inside for having yielded to the attraction of the wind, which this year was not sparing Casablanca in the slightest. The storm had come from the fringes of the Arabian desert, had swept across Sudan, Guinea, Mali, the Sahara. It was an oppressive wind that put great strain on the emotions—the neurons clashed together when it began to blow. Daoudi didn't recognize himself these last few days. If he'd chosen this line of work, it was because he'd counted on his cool, which had never let him down. Of course, people can escape the draw of Chergui, he thought to himself, but at times it can get horribly complicated. Above all, he'd realized that the death of Ichrak had affected him more than it should have. His whole flesh trembled at the thought of her; he understood with a feeling of terror that he would never again feel the fire he'd experienced when he stood in her presence. He moaned, like a child sobbing. What would he not have given to live it all again. He felt a violent spasm in his chest. He managed to get a grip on himself.

The first time he'd seen her was just after he'd been appointed inspector in the neighborhood. The new job was supposedly a promotion, but that wasn't how Daoudi saw it. Prior to that he'd been assigned to watch over tourist nuisances—bag snatching and the like—and he'd found ways to make good, either from the tourists themselves or from the culprit, so long as the latter had given proof of his skills, of course. The Derb Taliane and Cuba neighborhoods, where he worked now, were not so attractive to someone who wanted to move up in the world and improve his material comfort. The offenses committed there were small-time crimes: bag snatching, brawls, a stabbing from time to time. Not long ago some guy who'd finally been wrecked by alcohol had gotten hold of a sword and decided he was half ninja, half Scarface. He was threatening people along a whole stretch of his street. His buddies had intervened, gently at first, with *khouyas* and conciliatory gestures, palms upturned, but he'd disarmed one of them and injured him. There was no option but to send in Inspector Lahcen Choukri. Choukri turned up with a squad of five men. Two of them stopped the traffic; he posted the other three in a line right behind him, the way he'd seen in a video. In the middle of the street, arm held out horizontally, he aimed his finger at the perp and called out to him with a line from Booba's song "Take It Easy":

If you for real, you my prisoner, watch out!
If not, you my ho
There's dangers on the street
I got heat sweet and low, watch out!

The bold offender, unaware of who he was dealing with, or thinking he was in a rap battle, made as if to step forward, saying, "Fuck you!" like MC Jean Gab'1 in his hit song "Fuck You." Choukri didn't hesitate; he drew his gun and, faster than the ticket puncher of Lilas, sent two bullets into the madman's shoulder, quickly followed by one more in each leg, in this way avoiding killing him. Islam forbids drink, of course, but from there to executing a transgressor was a step that Mokhtar Daoudi's men never took in Derb Taliane. The inspector was proud of the discipline he'd instilled in his guys. In a word, all this was in the order of things, but it wasn't enough to feed a carnivore of the dimensions of Mokhtar Daoudi. The obvious compensation was that as chief of this station, he enjoyed absolute power; the men jumped to attention at his least movement, and he had a car provided. But above all it was the respect he was shown by the storekeepers of the neighborhood, which took the form of things that jangled or fluttered or did something else. It was inevitable, then, that he'd been shaken when he collided with Ichrak one day as he left his office. To his "Watch where you're going," the beautiful woman had replied with the greatest insolence: "You bump into me, and *I'm* supposed to apologize? Who do you think you are?"

This "Who do you think you are?" had stopped him in his tracks. The young woman had continued on her way, muttering an insult that he thought he caught.

"You there—come back!"

She stopped, but Daoudi had to take two or three steps toward her.

"Do you know who I am?"

"All I know is, you're someone who barreled into me and then was rude to me."

"I'm the new boss around here," said Daoudi, jerking his thumb behind him at the "Police Station" sign.

"So? That doesn't give you the right to do anything you want."

Mokhtar smiled. "Aren't you the brash one."

"I'm in a hurry, is what I am. I have to go."

The young woman turned on her heel and walked away. Mokhtar Daoudi watched her. She was wearing a fuchsia-colored gandoura. Her figure undulated like the heady smoke from a hookah. But her face, and above all the fiery look in her eye, haunted the detective from that moment. Her words had been disagreeable, but Daoudi relished the electric feeling she'd sent down his spine. She was a panther, and her bite made itself felt. Mokhtar liked strong characters of that kind. It was almost a provocation, addressed directly to him. Disillusioned on many fronts, on this one he had an endless fount of questions to keep his mind busy into the future. He knew he'd meet her again. Had he not been given the area he now controlled? This woman was a morsel fit for a king. He felt it; his detective's instinct whispered to his manhood that it was so.

～

Many men would have given their right arm to possess a woman of Ichrak's beauty, Daoudi continued in his thoughts.

With a temperament like that, they would have lost their heads over the murderous words that came out of her mouth. One reason that could have led to her death. For a being as impulsive and domineering as Guerrouj, a refusal could have constituted a perfectly valid motive to follow an action through to the end. He'd hesitated before replying to the question about where he'd been on the night of the murder, but the detective hadn't wanted to press him. There'd be time for that later. Nordine Guerrouj had quite a few interests around the edge of the old medina. He must have hit on Ichrak, given her looks. Tried to get her to work in his seedy bar, as he'd done with so many others. Daoudi knew that they knew each other. The young woman was bound to have brushed him off one day or another, and Nordine wasn't the kind of guy to let such a thing slide.

Had he met her that night? Or had it been someone else of his type? Somebody she'd maybe mouthed off to one time too often? Perhaps a conversation had taken a bad turn. The wound had looked like it was made by a knife dropping diagonally from above. The blade had sliced clean through the carotid artery and had slashed the top of her gandoura. After she'd been cut, she'd taken a few steps, as the blood spatter showed, and then collapsed at the bottom of the steps on Rue du Poète Taha Adnan, where her body had been found. Ichrak's character could provoke violent reactions. No one had succeeded in possessing her—the detective could bitterly attest to that himself. Ichrak drew men like an especially cruel idol, scorning anyone who might have the unfortunate idea of throwing themselves at her feet and worshiping her. For his part, Daoudi wished he'd never met her.

～

Sese was on edge. He was being let out of his cell. Like in a joke, his place was only a hundred yards away—he could just as easily have slept at home and clocked back in to the station in the morning. But for that to be allowed, you'd have to be a Sarkozy at the least. In the kingdom, such a privilege was unimaginable. The forty-eight-hour custody period should have ended at daybreak, but Daoudi didn't show up for work till around nine. Lieutenant Choukri had refused to release Sese before, claiming that the chief had taken the keys to the cell with him. On top of that, with his fists at his sides, he'd calmly recited to him: "Thirty months for sure inside / The joint is like your second home," from Booba's song "Lunatic." Sese was more than frustrated.

Rue Souss and Boulevard Sour Jdid, as far as the pump where the Red Cabs were beginning to gas up, had not waited for him in greeting the morning. The sun-drenched minaret of the Hassan II Mosque, in its lofty benevolence, along with the song of the muezzin drifting through the air, was a reminder of eternity, while clusters of people dotted the sidewalks, deep in conversation. It was clear that the day was only just beginning. Gestures were lazy; people were still in pajamas and house slippers or clad in fleece-lined gandouras with a zebra pattern. They were calculating, making plans to knot together the two ends of their daily lives. They asked each other if they were awake yet, inquired how they felt. They posed the same question half a dozen times, so as to be sure of the answer. Around a fruit and vegetable cart stationed at a corner, customers were sizing up the sweetest mandarins in the world, bunches of carrots, huge tomatoes, and potatoes. Children were swapping marbles like bookmakers, in preparation for the evening game that would take over the entire intersection. All-purpose stands—*ligablos,* as they were called in Kinshasa—attracted numerous customers buying bread and other breakfast items. Sese reached the covered terrace of the Café Jdid and kept walking.

"Hey, Sese, where've you been? No one's seen you for two days."

He didn't deign to reply. He'd just gotten out of the can and wasn't in the mood for banter. He muttered something inaudible and passed the terrace. His place was located behind the café, in front of which men were drinking tea and talking, playing cards or dominoes. Those who'd called out to him were busy arguing over their game.

"What's wrong? Have you stopped answering your buddies when they say hello?"

"Come off it, Mekloufi," said Si Miloud. "Leave him be. His friend just died—no wonder he doesn't feel like joking around. Don't hold it against him, Sese."

But the young man had already gone.

"Damn! She's dead?"

Mekloufi was lost in thought for a few seconds; then he went on: "You're right, Si Miloud, that girl deserves a minute's silence. Here I am kidding around, but when she passed in front of this terrace, *wallah*, who could even keep talking?"

And the minute of silence came about, purely at the mention of the dead woman. The swaying of Ichrak's hips had permanently marked the card players of the Café Jdid.

Si Miloud—the one who'd acted as mediator—had been a longtime civil servant in the Ministry of Justice, but he spent much of his retirement in the company of Mekloufi at the Jdid. The two of them were unlikely tablemates: Mekloufi had for years earned his living organizing convoys between the Ketama region and Marseilles, Paris, or Brussels. The hashish trade was a lucrative one, but he'd paid for it with various stretches in prison at home, and sometimes in Spain or in France. These setbacks had made him slow down and driven him to plan his retirement, after buying two or three apartments in the names of his wife and his children. The only risks he took these days were with cards in hand, sitting with Si Miloud and two other characters: Abdelwahed, a cab driver and confirmed bachelor who preferred to work by night and spend his days with the card players, and Ramdam, an old man, a little younger than Si Miloud, who owned an electrical supply store more or less opposite the café, which meant he was able to keep an eye on its comings and goings at his leisure. The terrace of the Café Jdid was not only a meeting place but also a prized observation post.

When Sese passed through the door to his dwelling, children descended upon him like a flock of sparrows. They belonged to his landlady, Mme Saïda Bouzid, widow of an army man, who rented out two rooms that looked onto the courtyard. "Stray bullet in Western Sahara," she'd said tersely on the subject of her late husband. The band of kids formed Sese's personal retinue when he was at home. They bugged him ceaselessly. It always took several attempts to get rid of them.

"Where've you been?" asked Mounia, the oldest. "Ihssan looked everywhere for you."

Sese turned toward his room, but he stopped and looked down at little Ihssan, who was watching him, a smile of joy on her lips, eyes shining. Sese couldn't resist and picked her up. His anger at Daoudi melted away at once.

Sese was alone in this country, and Mme Bouzid and her children were to some extent the family he lacked. There was Mounia, who was twelve or so; her brothers, Tawfik, ten, and Bilal, eight; and lastly Ihssan, four years old. She was Sese's favorite, and she adored him boundlessly, no doubt because of his dreads, in which she liked to bury her fingers.

"How are you, honey? Were you waiting for me?" The little girl nodded and at once took an interest in a braid of hair. "Here, look what I brought you." Sese offered her a candy that he took from his pocket. "Hang on, I'll unwrap it for you."

The moment the candy was in her hand, she popped it into her mouth.

"What about us?" the older ones shouted, laying siege to him. "Easy now! Here."

He gave each of them a treat. Since he'd been living there, the children would demand something—it could be anything at all—when he came back from his escapades, as proof that he'd been thinking of them during the day.

"Where were you, Sese?"

The young man turned to a woman with an ample body. Her loosened hair formed a black mane. This was the children's mother.

"I'll explain later, Lalah Saïda. I'm a bit tired."

Putting the little one down, he slipped away toward his room. The widow Bouzid followed him with her eyes, hands on hips, brows knitted, curious.

Let him rest, she thought to herself. He needs it. He'll tell me himself.

"Come on, it's you to play. What are you daydreaming about?"

"Daydreaming? Have you no heart? I can't get anything down!" Mekloufi exclaimed, holding his throat between thumb and index finger. "This tea, for instance," he went on, "I can't even take a sip of it anymore. *Miskina!* The poor woman! I'm gone for three days visiting my cousin in Rabat; I come back, and we're playing away like nothing happened. If Sese hadn't come by, I'd be the only person in Cuba and Derb Taliane not to know about the girl. Dead! And she was murdered, what's more?"

"It slipped our minds," Si Miloud came back. "But don't jump to conclusions; we don't know for sure if it was murder. It might just have been an accident. The case is under investigation; we should let justice take its course. Besides, with the life she led, I'm not that surprised."

"The life she led? It's not your job to assign life and death, Miloud. Let God be the judge of that," Mekloufi retorted.

"What could she have done not to lead that life?" said Abdelwahed. "You saw her figure. When she walked, you'd think—"

"Have some respect for the dead," Ramdam broke in. He'd lived in the neighborhood forever. "Don't talk of her like that. You're too young; you don't know anything. Her mother is where it all began. She's only the result. If you think Ichrak was beautiful, you should have seen her mother in all her glory. You reckon Ichrak was uncontrollable? You've no idea if you never met Zahira. When the urge took her, she'd run barefoot through the streets of the medina, cursing anyone who dared look at her. Because, among those who despised her, some had been in her bed. Many were terrified that one day she'd spill the beans to the whole world. When Ichrak was born, who would have been crazy enough to admit he'd been with a madwoman who ran about exposed to the elements? Because of that, no one can say who her father was. True, there are suspicions about certain people . . ."

"Have they arrested anyone yet?"

"Are you kidding? A girl like that does nothing but attract enemies. She was too quick by half with her tongue," Si Miloud said. "If you ask me, they'll be looking for a long time. On top of that, these are difficult times. As you all know, I have some experience with justice; I've looked into the matter, and I can assure you of one thing: Chergui has never blown the way it's been blowing these last days in Casa. We've never seen anything like it before."

"It's true," agreed Ramdam. "I'm sensitive to these things, and I feel it, I'm telling you."

"Sensitive, you? Come off it. Have you seen the price of a yard of cable in your store?" laughed Abdelwahed.

"That's got nothing to do with anything. I *am* sensitive. Even my wife is less sweet because of Chergui. She's nagging me about everything: money for this, money for that, money for the house, for the kids—"

"Don't laugh; he's right," said Si Miloud. "So you reckon the girl was murdered?"

He was silent for a moment, then looked each of the others in the eye, and said, "And none of you has wondered to what extent this wind is responsible? It can drive people mad. In fact, there have been stranger cases. A few years ago there was one, at the courthouse in Marrakech. I wasn't there, but I heard about it."

"You're going to tell us some old nonsense. Play your card!" said Mekloufi.

"Me, talk nonsense? Excuse me, I've studied. I've been to college."

"So have I," retorted Mekloufi. "What do you think?"

"College? Where?"

"In France. At Baumettes." That was the prison in Marseilles. "I was smart. I took advantage of this program when I was banged up there."

At the look of dismay from Si Miloud and the others, he responded, "What?"

"You're right; I'd rather play than hear that. But I already went; it's your turn."

3

CLOUDS

IN DERB TALIANE, the alleyways crisscross all the way to the medina and offer nothing but surprises. They form a tangle of passages that curve unexpectedly or grow narrow without warning. The right angles called for by the rules of city planning are nowhere in evidence here. To enter among these streets, you need a compass and a visa, a confident and, at the same time, reassuring mien. Despite the anarchic layout, there are patterns in ways of thinking. It's rare to find the green and white of the Raja Club Athletic on a wall, because here the red and blue of the Wydad Athletic Club of Casablanca holds sway. The only other soccer clubs acknowledged in the neighborhood are those whose logo is printed on T-shirts in the factories of the Aïn-Sebaâ industrial zone: Barcelona, PSG, AC Milan . . .

The day Ichrak met Sese for the first time, after she left him she took one of those alleyways lined with many colors, then entered a maze encircled by lofty blue-painted walls, with occasional windows or doors. The light coming from high up and reflecting against the blue made you feel like you were following a path toward some kind of sky.

"What a strange guy," she said to herself with a smile as she thought of the young Congolese. He'd been a bit too bold for her liking, but he'd intrigued her to the point of wheedling her phone number out of her. Ichrak couldn't figure out how he'd managed to do it. She'd trusted him from the start, which was not her usual way—no doubt it was because he'd lied with such conviction. And then that business of cyberseduction—how could he have suggested such a thing to her? She told herself that if she saw him again, next time she wouldn't fall for his little game, but right away she remembered the expression on his face as he recited his funny little poem about "sticking to it," and she couldn't help laughing inside. Trying to suppress her smile, she pushed open the door of her place, which was also sky blue. She entered a room in which a middle-aged woman was asleep on a sofa bed against the wall.

"*Ima?* Mother?"

The woman didn't move. Her breathing was regular. The little living room had a single window that looked out onto a staircase leading to the rooftop terrace. Openings near the ceiling brought in a little more light. Ichrak went into a bedroom, where a large mattress lay on the floor. Dusk had fallen, and she lit a lamp covered with a piece of orange-tinted transparent fabric. She burned a little *thiouraye* incense; then, opening a zipper, she pulled her brightly colored robe over her head in a single movement and unhooked her bra. The lamp threw tangerine-colored shadows on the walls and the objects in the room. Slipping into a lighter gown of fine white cotton and loosening her hair, Ichrak dropped onto the mattress and reached for her leather purse. She took out her MP3 player and put in her earphones. Lowering her head onto the cushions, she pressed Play.

In the reflection of the shop windows, I saw myself placing my steps in the steps of that man, my handbag brushing against my hip. He was speaking to me, and I was nodding. I saw his lips move, I heard the sound of his voice, but I could not understand the meaning of the words he was uttering. My entire attention was focused on my chest. I could feel my heart beating, swelling, filling with some substance that was heavy, that burned, and this substance was spreading through my whole body.

Ichrak was soon swept away by the text. The actress's voice was solemn, the words were pronounced precisely, but at times emotion affected her delivery, which sped up. Ichrak liked to yield to the melody of the words. The flow of the sentences was a thread she could follow blindly, expecting nothing but wonder. Even if at times she didn't fully understand, the spirit conveyed by the text was more than enough. Little by little these journeys through immateriality had become essential in Ichrak's life. She could lose herself for hours listening to the voice. She knew certain passages by heart and repeated them aloud or in her mind, the way you'd do with a prayer. At a certain moment, she pulled out the earphones instinctively. Her mother had woken up in the next room.

"Ichrak!"

"Go back to sleep, Mama; I'm tired."

Ichrak laid her head back down. The last few days, her mother had been taking her medication; she was doing well. Zahira had never been quite right in her head, but with age and the onset of diabetes, her mind had gone into a tailspin, and she'd developed a kind of schizophrenia that her daughter found completely bewildering. Zahira had become a different person. She would turn violent, at which point nothing but venom would come from her mouth. The cruelty of her words wounded Ichrak for days on end and merely intensified the questions to which she'd been seeking answers since she was born. To prevent these crises, she needed to give her mother a certain regular medication. The stuff was expensive; it swallowed up everything she earned. Recently it seemed as if the sickness was worsening. The ancients used to say that when Chergui showed itself, it was best not to go out, not to breathe or even listen, at times, for fear of attracting some misfortune. Ichrak wasn't superstitious, but her mother's condition worried her more and more. How much longer could it go on?

The box she'd been carrying contained small paper sacks—plastic bags had recently been banned by laws aimed at protecting the environment—and she was about to go sell them to her usual clients, the traders of the medina. She would make the rounds of the narrow streets overrun with shoppers and tourists. She'd hope to turn a least a slight profit. As a teenager, Ichrak, who was a born leader, had formed commando teams of children washing the windows of cars stopped at red lights. The business came to an end when there was a crackdown on children clinging to the windshields. Afterward it was plastic sacks, packets of paper tissues. These days, when the opportunity arose, she sometimes worked as a day laborer in an industrial park, packing products that she herself could never afford.

The woman in the living room groaned out something unintelligible and started mumbling. Ichrak put her earphones in and plunged back into the story at the moment where the woman of *At the Origin Our Obscure Father* had begun to recall her lover:

> *For a long while he moved his hands through my hair; then he placed his palm on the back of my head, pressing ever so lightly, and this simple gesture relieved, for a while, the pain I was feeling. He sensed it, and so he continued to do it as I lay against him, my arms around his neck and his so-heavy body. He was under my body, under my scent, under my sway; it was stronger*

than him, he said. At that moment, he could not be anywhere
else but under me; he said more, more.

~

In Mokhtar Daoudi's book, being a cop in Casablanca was
trickier than being one elsewhere because the standard of living
was very high in the city. If you didn't display signs of wealth,
you could easily be taken for a hick, and nobody wanted to deal
with that kind of person. In the matter of poor Ichrak, the inspector didn't stand to gain a single dirham, but he had to do his
duty, and Guerrouj had become a priority from the moment he'd
lied to Daoudi when he'd been pinned down outside the bar. The
inspector was wondering if he could make something out of
that. Why was the guy being so coy about where he'd been, if he
had nothing to feel guilty about? The detective had decided to
dig a little. Information also meant power. He wanted to know
who Guerrouj met with and why. Daoudi always managed to dig
deep into any case that came along. As concerned this investigation, despite his involvement he'd also experienced Ichrak's
brutal death as a relief. There had been a day, or rather a night,
when she'd been a witness to his weakness. It was good that she
was gone. In front of anyone else, Inspector Mokhtar Daoudi
could have put on an act, but with Ichrak it was impossible. She'd
marked him for good.

His patience was rewarded; Nordine Guerrouj came out of
his bar, swaying slightly, and headed for his metallic-blue Series
3. He got in and pulled away from his parking spot with two
abrupt tugs of the wheel. He drove for a short distance, then sig-
naled left, made a U-turn, and headed for Place des Nations
Unies. Nordine was moving at a fair clip, but the Dacia caught up
with him at the lights. When he set off again, he went toward the
ultramodern building of the Casaport Station, turned left, drove
for a couple hundred yards, stopped opposite the cannon

adorning the terrace of the La Sqala restaurant, and parked on the median. Daoudi pulled up too, a little farther back, and killed his lights.

From a white Class A parked amid other cars, a woman got out. She was wearing high heels and a close-fitting black dress. She walked toward the Beemer, opened the door, and got in. Daoudi was relatively far away, but he recognized the figure of Farida Azzouz. The car set off again toward the Corniche that ran along the coast, left the Grand Mosque to its right, and headed out in the direction of Ain Diab. At a certain point, it turned right toward a lighthouse that shone upon the sea. Otherwise, things were pretty dark all around. The road was under repair, and there was a lot of construction in the neighborhood, but some luxury restaurants had opened, as shown by the makes of the cars parked left, right, and center. In front of the Cabestan, Nordine looked for a discreet spot, parked, and turned off his lights.

Darkness came in handy sometimes. Under its cover, the possibilities were limitless. Not much could be seen in it, unless one was like a cat and could make out things and people in the shadows. That was what Nordine Guerrouj was thinking as he sat in his car right next to Farida Azzouz. He put his ability to see in the dark to use and took a good look at the woman as if offering himself a gift. Her hair was jet black, thick, shoulder length, carefully arranged; one strand was tucked behind her ear, revealing a cluster of diamonds. Her bronzed skin glowed like the morning sun. Her perfectly harmonious features were accentuated by large dark-brown eyes, dotted with gold and graced with infinitely long lashes, above a short nose and a mouth whose lower lip was fleshy as a fruit and whose beauty was brought out by scarlet Dior lipstick. But Farida also had a sensibility that was as contagious as fever, especially when, as now, closeness was being turned into a mode of doing business. The tinted windows helped to heighten the sense of intimacy, and a heady perfume filled the vehicle to feed any dizziness that might be produced, should the need arise. Nordine's eyes had left Farida's face; he was now staring at her thighs. With age—she'd turned forty—they had grown heavier, but they seemed to have gained in strength; a man would need a powerful body to sustain the weight. Nordine's senses awoke in a natural, effortless way, like at the height of the rut. The alcohol he'd drunk contributed to his state. He tried to stay focused, but Farida's voice swept him away, as if on velvet, into a kind of irreality composed of peril and sensuality, even though he remembered the need to stick to his guns—otherwise, she would eat him alive.

"Tell me about Rue Goulmima, Nordine."

It was the same thing every time. She only had to open her mouth, and Nordine felt himself capsizing. Farida was well aware of the charm she exerted and used it extravagantly. She sat up a little, pulling her thighs closer together and letting the diffuse light play on her softly gleaming skin. There was a silence. Nordine Guerrouj ended it: "I've set things in motion there. A bit more pressure and we'll soon be rid of all the vermin squatting on your property. I made you a promise, and I'll keep it. You're getting to know me."

"I want to know you more, Nordine. I have to recover what's mine. I'm losing money daily with these people. It all needs to be cleared and demolished. I need a completely empty site."

Farida pronounced the last sentence almost in a whisper. Nordine Guerrouj saw her chest rise and fall to the rhythm of her breathing and of some passion she was trying to hide. He realized that he needed to shift gears. The patience of those he worked for was being stretched to its limits.

Nordine had succeeded in evicting many of the residents, but there were some holdouts who were still in occupation and were refusing to leave. Up till now, threats had not worked. The property to be recovered had enabled Farida to do well but also, in view of her ambitions, to acquire a certain power through a network she'd built using a blend of intelligence and charm combined with an utter unwillingness to compromise. She was dangerous, and Nordine knew it. He recognized the familiar feeling, especially when it was accompanied with a rush of adrenaline. Nordine Guerrouj observed Farida, his eyes half closed, the skin around his scar pulled taut. His gaze rose back up to her face for a little relief but then dropped again to the shoulders, which were shown off to advantage by her black silk Prada dress with its broad neckline that could faintly be discerned plunging steeply down her back, baring an expanse of smooth hot skin on which Nordine dreamed of placing the flat of his hand so as to leave a mark of power and constraint.

They talked some more about property ownership and evictions, but it was only a front, because Nordine was now thinking about how he felt and had begun to focus on Chergui, which was blowing like never before, putting him into a strange state, as if it personally had it in for him and him alone. He experienced a constant rage in his heart, with a desire to bite, to tear things with his hands. He longed for it to stop. He could tell that Farida too had been unable to escape its influence. The sandstorms that had blown up in recent days plagued her like jealous lovers. She managed to control it in the daytime, but she couldn't sleep, finding herself unable to calm a mind assailed by all kinds of thoughts that sometimes burned her flesh. As for her heart, it beat much too strongly, and she felt herself suffocating, or so she claimed, a hand with lacquered nails resting softly against one breast. The words spoken between the woman and the crook were of little importance; what counted was all that was implied. For Nordine, the crucial thing was to prolong the kind of truce that was generating so many emotions in the very air they breathed. He liked to arm-wrestle with himself. He gritted his teeth as he yielded to the delights of words that were suggested but could not be uttered.

For Farida, what mattered was the breath with which each sentence left her mouth. Experience had taught her that it was like an invisible love potion, whose effectiveness she was well aware of, for she felt with extraordinary force Nordine Guerrouj's gaze on her chest and the effort he was making to control himself. Unknown to him, she was making him surpass himself, offering him the sight of the silk shimmering on her thighs, but also of her knees, which she parted slightly. The gap was not enough to dare to slip a hand in but sufficient to render shadow, darkness, heat. An ungaugeable stretch of time passed in this way, in a perfect simulacrum of immobility on both sides, till eventually Guerrouj pulled out and drove Farida back to her car. During the journey, not one word was exchanged; the silence alone spoke.

"I have to go now, Nordine."

They'd arrived. Farida opened the car door, put one foot in its Giuseppe Zanotti sandal on the ground, and added: "Next time bring me better news, understand?"

She broke off, her gaze intensified, and she went on: "Watch out for Chergui. It can drive you mad, but it begins by tormenting you. Like now. Have a nice night, Nordine."

She closed the door and walked to her vehicle.

The stakes justified the effort, Nordine Guerrouj was thinking. It was a matter of money, but also of having her, Farida. She was the kind of woman that fell for bastards like him. He'd felt it the first time he saw her, and it was natural, because she needed such men to do her dirty work. With her he'd become like one of those fierce male pythons that foolishly let themselves be tracked down and killed by a female hunter, because they suddenly find themselves weakened and tamed by their own hormones and by the pheromones the woman emits. He would do anything, then, to satisfy an ego that was telling him to conquer her.

The other side of this business was more problematic. Nordine had sent his henchmen to intimidate the tenants in Farida's apartment buildings on Rue Goulmima. Since the great period of migrations, the city had been invaded by Africans from all over: Senegal, Mali, Gambia, Cameroon, and even further, from the two Congos. Early on they'd settled in like termites, and everyone knows those things don't leave their nest until they themselves decide to. The value of the buildings had plummeted, and the property had to be made profitable to ensure a minimum upkeep. Nordine was responsible for the financial part, which is to say, obliging the immigrants to pay their paltry rents. He knew how to make himself indispensable to Farida; she owned virtually an entire block of buildings, whose expenses could increase very rapidly. Ideally the neighborhood would be included in a larger urban-planning project, but for the time being, at least, the public authorities weren't involved. At this impasse, the Saudi Saqr Al-Jasser had appeared with a plan and an offer to buy, and now Nordine had to put his gray cells to work a bit more effectively: the tenants needed to be kicked out as quickly as possible so the bulldozers could go to work. When the law doesn't allow it, you have to turn to people like Nordine Guerrouj. Al-Jasser was demanding land freed of any construction so he could build a luxury complex with a five-star hotel, convention center, shopping mall, and pedestrian precinct. But to obtain the relevant permits, they first had to show that the buildings were unoccupied. It was Nordine's job to bring this about without making too many waves.

4

PARTICULATE MATTER

FOR A MOMENT NOW, Ichrak had stopped asking herself why she was sitting in this car, next to this man in the driving seat. She was feeling simply that she was where she should be, without really understanding what that meant. Despite its immensity, the sprawling city had not prevented her and Cherkaoui from finding each other, because when two beings are destined to know one another, even if the world is not small, their enthusiasms, their ambitions, can be of such scope that they'll cross paths whatever the circumstances might be. Through the windshield, they could see the hood of the Peugeot 5008 SUV following its route briskly, changing lanes, almost touching fenders with others that were doing the same thing. The number of vehicles made it seem as if they were in a traffic jam, but one that was moving at great speed. The car went down Boulevard Mohamed Zerktouni. After passing the Twin Center, it had left behind Anfa, Ziraoui, and Ben Kadour Boulevards. In a megacity like Casa, if you want to travel quickly, you have to set aside the highway code from time to time, but unanimously, which always creates the appearance of synchronization: a certain tenuous fluidity would arise despite everything. The SUV came to the end of

Boulevard Aïn Taoujtate, turned left onto Avenue de Nice, then took Avenue TanTan in the well-to-do neighborhood of Bourgogne. Cherkaoui was focusing on his driving. The windows were open, and Ichrak, eyes closed, was letting the air caress her face. They soon arrived in Rue Cénacles des Solitudes.

If the first meeting between Ichrak and Cherkaoui had been by chance, no one could have predicted that a second would prove possible in a city of three million inhabitants. But in the crowd thronging the sidewalks along boulevards lined with apartment buildings that reflected shadow and sunlight, Ichrak had immediately recognized the stranger she'd met some time before in front of a theater. He did too. Among all the faces, that of the young woman had leaped out at him. Their smiles spoke volumes about how pleased they were to see each other again. Cherkaoui had suggested going to get something to eat and had taken her to a Tacos de Lyon on Boulevard Mohamed Zerktouni. They'd had a long conversation interspersed with laughter, like old friends. Ichrak felt at ease in a way she rarely did. Without knowing why, he'd sensed that he would see her again often. As he left, he'd asked for her phone number and had put his own into the young woman's phone. Their subsequent meetings had reinforced Ichrak's feeling of trust, and she'd unburdened herself on the subject of her everyday difficulties, her mother's illness, though without overstepping the bounds of decency, and she'd spoken of that which was hidden within her. Cherkaoui taught her things she didn't know about life, about his travels and people he'd met, and had asked her questions about herself, but without ever behaving like the majority of men. At the same time, Ichrak wondered what he wanted of her. He seemed interested in her life, in any case, sometimes in tiny details, like how her day had gone, from getting up to eating supper. Or how she'd spent her time when she was small. Had she gone to school? It was as if he were trying to piece together a puzzle. She knew he was the director of the Espace des Amdiaz theater company, and no doubt that occupation gave him an open mind. Perhaps too, since he met many women in his line of work, he didn't hit on every one. All the same, Ichrak didn't really understand his motivations.

Neither did Cherkaoui, in fact. Over sixty, he didn't ask himself what he liked so much about Ichrak. He knew many women, but Ichrak's naturalness and candor made her different from the young actresses and pseudointellectual ladies who dotted his life. At his age he'd seen it all. He'd been married to Farida for twenty-five years, and she no longer inspired him to lay the world at her feet. She was a live coal, and when a man wanted to win her, she let him know that it took more than a garden variety fire iron to make her burst into flames. This attitude had always drawn men to her. Today, Cherkaoui was quite simply tired of chasing around after her. Her vast material independence had in the end come between them; when she was taking care of business matters, her time was exclusively her own. The fact that they'd grown apart was merely something to be acknowledged; it didn't bother him any more than that, since he didn't know what he could do about it. With Ichrak he could relax.

Sitting in an armchair, he watched her. She lay on the bed, at times adopting a pose that could be seen as suggestive. But it didn't bother him; in fact, it reassured him.

"Why did you bring me here?"

"This is my place. It's just a little studio apartment adjoining the big house you saw, which doesn't belong to me. But what you see here is mine. My father bought it for me after college, so I could live my own life. I kept it, and I come here often; it's quiet around here. It's modest but comfortable."

Indeed, the apartment mostly consisted of one large room with a huge bed in the corner, along with a wardrobe, a chest of drawers, chairs, and a long table. A door off the hallway led to the bathroom.

"So this is where you bring your women—is that what you mean?"

He didn't answer. The moment she'd crossed the threshold, Ichrak had dropped her purse on an armchair, sent her flats skittering across the tiled floor, undone the royal-blue turban that matched her dress, and thrown herself down on the bed. Lying on her side, head propped on a hand, a sarcastic smile on her lips, she was staring at Cherkaoui, who sat, legs crossed, on the armchair facing her.

"It's more discreet too. I'm married, don't forget, and my wife is a hellcat; she'll find out quickly enough about our rendezvous. I don't want to cause problems for you, or for myself either, but stopping seeing you is out of the question! It's been a while. I called you several times."

"I know, Si Ahmed. I saw the missed calls."

"Is everything OK?"

"No. It's my mother. And work. But mostly Mother. I wanted to talk to you about that, Si Ahmed. I need money, for her, for her medication, and I can't manage any longer. If you could help me . . ."

"Don't worry; we'll take care of it."

"I'm worried about her health; she's getting worse every day. Soon I'll end up as mad as she is."

Ichrak stared harder at Cherkaoui.

"Tell me, Si Ahmed: the first time we met, you asked me if I was the daughter of Zahira. Do you know her?"

"Everyone does."

"You're not everyone. You're not from the same circles, you and her. When could you have met her? Where? When you were young?"

Cherkaoui said nothing for a moment.

"I knew her like everyone did, Ichrak. What do you want to know?"

"About her youth, her experiences. I've heard a lot, but I want to know more."

"You know . . ." Cherkaoui hesitated. "She was very beautiful, your mother. Yes, and with a particular kind of beauty. Like you, as it happens. But she was . . . She was completely uncontrollable."

Strange, Ichrak thought to herself. When it's about my mother, Cherkaoui—a literary man—has to search for words. He definitely wasn't telling her everything he knew about her mother.

"What, or who, was it that drove her mad?"

He didn't answer. There was a silence. Ichrak wasn't saying everything either. She didn't mention that in seeking traces of her mother, she was above all looking into her own origins, the piece of herself that was missing. The father she had never known. She found the situation outrageous—no one told her anything, as though Derb Taliane and the entire city had lost its memory. It was as if her past had been obliterated.

In the end Cherkaoui replied, "Sometimes life itself makes us lose our reason. But you must know more about it than I do, right?"

"More than you? If I did, I wouldn't be here begging for what belongs to me."

It was the same thing every time: a wall of silence when she wanted to know. Cherkaoui seemed fond of her, but he reacted like everyone else. Unless she was imagining it. Fine, but how did they not know, when everyone knew everything about everybody? Could her mother be the only exception? Exasperated, Ichrak asked, "What if your wife finds out we've been meeting?"

"I'll tell her the truth."

"What truth?"

"That I look upon you as a friend."

"A friend? And she'll believe you just like that, take you at your word?" The young woman burst out laughing.

"Don't laugh!"

Ichrak stopped in surprise. Cherkaoui's expression had suddenly become serious, his voice hard: "Why would she not believe me? Anything else between you and me would be . . . It would be inappropriate," he concluded firmly.

In this he had once again sought his words and had betrayed his age. Ichrak didn't know why, but she believed him. And his answer reassured her. Ever since she'd known Cherkaoui, when she was with him she felt safe, and she yielded to that feeling more than she had ever done before. He paid for her dinners, treated her with courtesy. Without a second thought, she'd even agreed to come to this room with him, and she hadn't felt the least bit apprehensive. Nor did she feel the aversion she usually had toward men. He acted like they did, but she didn't regard him as a man. She didn't understand this phenomenon. It was the first time she'd ever experienced it.

Outside, Casablanca was breathing to the rhythm of the pistons in the car engines, but not in here. Silence took over the space for several long minutes. Nothing could be heard. The light filtering through the half-closed shutters lay in blurry strips against the wall. Ichrak and Cherkaoui were each lost in themselves. They evidently had nothing else to share with one another. There are times for saying things, but moments devoted to introspection should be experienced in tranquility; this suited them both perfectly, and the instant lingered of its own accord, making the ether lighter and ever less oppressive.

⁓

What Ichrak hated more than anything were guys that wouldn't leave you alone. After she met Sese, she'd thought that she only had herself to blame; you don't just give your phone number out like that to the first comer. She'd given in and agreed to take a glass of tea on the covered terrace of the Café Jdid on Boulevard Sour Jdid, near Sese's. The card players pretended not to notice anything when the two young people showed up.

"Salaam alaikum!" Sese called.

"Salaam," Mekloufi murmured vaguely.

The new arrivals sat down a couple of tables away.

"See, that's where I live," said Sese, pointing toward the door that led to Mme Bouzid's courtyard. "It's also where I work. I'll show you later."

"We're staying here. I'm not going to your place."

"Who do you take me for?"

"I know what you men are like."

"Over there," he went on, still indicating the door, "it's nothing but business. It's money—dough, moolah, ackers. But you have to know where to look for it. I thought some more about my proposal. The Western seduction boom is imploding. Since the last time we spoke, it's gotten even worse. Speed is called for. So then, my sister—can I call you my sister?"

"Whatever."

"What would you like?"

Sese turned to the server, who only had eyes for Ichrak.

"Two teas please, Rachid."

"Two teas?"

After a moment during which he stood there without moving, he repeated once again, "You said two teas, right?"

Any way of buying time was good. It was plain that his eyes, and all his other parts, were having a hard time parting from Sese's companion. In the end, in despair he was forced to move off and return to his duties.

"I was saying, you must know that you're a knockout. If the guys that voted for the seven wonders of the world were still alive, you'd be the eighth. Women like you, I've been all over

Africa, and I have to say that since I left Kinshasa, you're the one that's made the biggest impression on me. In Europe there's all those Kate Mosses and what have you, but they don't have what you have. Over there that doesn't even exist, eyes and a body like yours; I'm certain of it."

"Are you starting again?"

"Not at all! What I mean is that in front of a screen, you could generate sums you can't even imagine."

"Are you trying to get me to do filthy stuff?"

"No, there's no need. That can be left to others. Listen, I have experience in these things, yet still when I saw you, it was beyond me. Can you imagine some guy in Paris or Brussels or Geneva? Where they speak French? In any case, all the advertising we need has been floating around in the West for years, and it's totally free. No one has that kind of publicity available, not even Nike or Adidas. Coca-Cola's PR is nothing compared to ours. Since 9/11 all they talk about is the Arab-Islamic world. The Arabs this, the Arabs that. The *Titanic*? The American Civil War? It was the Arabs. Hiroshima, Fukushima? Totally their doing. Climate change? No need to even ask. Even the Soissons Vase—ask Sarkozy who broke it, and he'll tell you: the guy must have been an Arab. Same goes for the one that lit the fire under Joan of Arc, according to some people in France. But for all that, on the TV there are only ever men with beards. To the point that it's the in thing, all over the world. There are planeloads of them. The few Arab or Maghrebi women they show are all wearing the veil! They're trying to hide them from us! It has to stop. Just imagine then: you appear, kohl, embroidered gown, the works. With your exceptional beauty, all you'll have to say is hello."

One of Ichrak's eyebrows had gone up in the middle of Sese's pitch.

"You're crazy. You watch too many movies on that computer of yours. I've never heard about any of this before."

"Don't worry; we'll both be close to the screen. You'll be on for a bit; then I'll introduce myself, make my presentation, and have them go to the payment page."

"How do you mean?"

"You think they're just going to sit there once they see you? They won't be able to. They'll do things . . . You don't know these types. We take a picture, and I explain it all with a screenshot in my hand."

"Blackmail? I don't do that sort of thing."

"Not at all, it's just a matter of being persuasive."

"Like I said, you're nuts. Off your rocker."

For his part, Sese wasn't the kind of person to let something go once he had an idea in his head. He and Ichrak met several times more in the medina, but Sese stopped going on about her beauty. He dwelled rather on the quality of her voice, on her talent for storytelling, and above all, even if she didn't yet realize it, on her talent for teamwork, which was proving to be remarkable and ought to be nurtured. He kept it up till one day Ichrak said, "I'll come."

~

"Well now, *sœur na ngai*—my sister!"

"There's more if you want it."

The widow Bouzid had just brought a plate of chicken and plum tagine, knowing it was a favorite of Sese's.

"Lalah Saïda, it's too much."

"You know, the first time you came to ask about renting the room, I agreed right away because you said you were from Zaire. You didn't say 'from Congo,' like the others. It reminded me of my late husband, who talked about Zaire all the time, even though he'd not spent that much time there."

"Was that when Mobutu put down the Katanga rebellion with the aid of the valiant troops of Hassan II?"

"No, it was a different time. During the war over the Aozou Strip in Chad. Your army was fighting alongside Hissène Habré against Gaddafi's army. Some Libyan prisoners had been sent to Kinshasa, and my husband was one of the Moroccan military who were detailed to bring them here, so the king could send them home safely. For Gaddafi, prisoners were cowards who ought to be killed. My poor husband always told me that Zaire was a very beautiful country and that the people were so nice. You are too, Sese. The children adore you, especially little Ihssan."

She turned her head.

"Ah, good morning, Monsieur Derwich!"

The adjacent door had just opened, and Slimane Derwich, who taught literature at the local university, seemed to be waiting for someone on his doorstep. He didn't reply. The street door opened, and a slender young woman came in. She was wearing a long close-fitting white skirt, an assortment of diaphanous peach-colored fabrics, and a scarf in the same color. When she noticed Mme Bouzid, her face lit up in a smile.

"Good morning," she said.

She moved toward Monsieur Derwich and greeted him too. After frowning in the direction of Sese and Mme Bouzid, Derwich let her in and closed the door.

Inside the room, the heavy heat of the outside could be felt, along with the glare of the sun on the houses, pressing shadows flat against the walls, keeping people cloistered helplessly in their homes. Young Noor had sat down on a chair, her slim hands crossed upon a book and a notepad that she'd placed in her lap. She looked askance toward the window. The scarf, one of whose ends passed under her chin and fell down her back, underlined her reserve. Slimane Derwich, at his desk, was just finishing some work on his computer. Aside from the continuous hum always in the air in large cities, and the clicking of keys, silence reigned. Between these four walls it had a particular quality. It was a silence filled with undulations, with nuances of texture, and it hung oppressively in the cramped space. When Slimane decided he was done, he turned his chair toward the young woman. His posture was as usual stiff and unmoving, and his eyes, far from Noor's, seemed to be searching for words to begin the conversation. She took the initiative:

"Thank you, Monsieur Slimane. It's generous of you to meet with me during your free time."

"It's only to be expected," mumbled the teacher. "When it happens that one of my students—a brilliant one, to boot—needs a little help, I cannot but shoulder my responsibilities and come to her assistance."

The words had come out mechanically, but it had given him time to recover his wits. Because he needed that, did Slimane. He never should have asked her to come like this, to his place. He could have offered her lessons on campus, in a vacant classroom, just the two of them. But when she'd come to see him, looking him straight in the eye and expressing candidly her need to gain a better understanding of the work of Assia Djebar, he had mentioned that he was beginning research for a monograph on that writer and stated that the subject couldn't be dealt with in five minutes. He'd suggested private lessons at his home, and before he had time to regret saying it, he heard his student say yes. She'd had to repeat her subsequent question twice:

"What's your address? I'll come by whenever it's convenient for you."

It has to be said that that was the last thing he'd expected from Noor. Girls constituted the great majority in his classes. He was aware that some of them sought to seduce him in a nice sort of way and that they used all kinds of wiles to do so. But Noor had never played that game. She was his best student, the most hardworking; she took copious notes, frowning in concentration behind the lenses of her frameless glasses. Today she wasn't wearing them; it was the first time he could actually see her eyes. Despite her discretion, Noor had long attracted his attention. Because of her gracefulness, firstly. She was like a liana in movement, every gesture breathing refinement. She was less ostentatious than her classmates yet more vibrant than them. Most of the time her presence unsettled Slimane Derwich, and it was a struggle to ensure that his lectures remained coherent from sentence to sentence.

"I'm delighted that you've taken an interest in Assia Djebar. I see you've brought *Woman without Sepulcher*. An excellent choice. Is there a passage that speaks to you especially? I'd like to know how you feel toward the author."

"Would you like me to read? You don't mind?"

"Not at all."

"I'll read two or three pages. You're sure?"

"Go ahead."

The young woman smiled, opened the volume at a bookmarked page, cleared her throat, and began to read.

You're lucky to be a mother with a family, especially in this small town where everyone knows each other!

In this so intimate place, the young woman's voice sounded different than usual. Slimane frowned to try and stay focused and strove to attend to every word.

I would lift up my headscarf, which had slipped down onto my shoulders; I would put it back on my head, would imprison my hair once again! I would even grip the ends of the fabric in my teeth. I'd hold the gauze face covering in my hand. Then I would go out, the veil of silk and wool enveloping my entire body. I would set off down gray hallways where the police officers stared at me, often with a hostile eye, as they unceremoniously manhandled teenage suspects or older peasants toward the cells. I would pace up and down, a lone figure.

Slimane had already stopped paying attention. Not for lack of interest in the story but because the pressure was too great. The voice—which for the first time was intended for him and him alone and was emerging from a body that was right there, inches away—bound him as if in a spell. The words barely reached his ears. They seemed to become diluted in the air along with the light flowery fragrance with which the young woman was enveloped.

Veiled in this way, like a peasant rather than a city dweller, I who was after all the widow of the crooked storekeeper El Hadj, who everyone in my neighborhood would recognize ... El Hadj, killed in the scrub a few weeks earlier. I returned to the alleyways of my neighborhood, where the stores had already closed.

He became aware of his distracted state when the young woman stopped reading.

"Go on," he said, to make it seem as if he was listening.

I started to talk, during the following two months. In all the cross-examinations for which he brought me in at the last minute (each time, a double knock at the door: urgent summons). I should have asked myself: what woman, one day in this town, had ever had to go "urgently" to a lover who she knew would almost certainly leave her dead, or forgotten, or, worse, reviled by all, in his wake?

During the entire narration of Zoulikha's extraordinary fate, Slimane Derwich was not thinking about Assia Djebar's depiction of women. Because of the subtle perfume emanating from Noor's clothing and her skin, he was no longer thinking about the book but, once again, was in the presence of the young woman, among words that seemed to glide over him. It wasn't that his IQ had taken a nosedive; it hadn't changed one bit. It had just reformed lower down, in the gray regions of his reptilian brain. The young woman's bearing and her reserve made no difference. Listening to the phrasing, read with such sensitivity, affected him only moderately; he was subject to his own semantics alone now. How could a passage from a book have retained its rigor and its poetry when Slimane Derwich himself was plunged in complete metonymy, in a sort of mise en abyme of his own composition? What he heard could no longer have so much meaning now he was wrapped in pheromones from the perfume of the troubling Noor. More stirring than usual, his student was not helping in the least to release him from the libidinous syntax his psyche was thrusting him into.

It was warmer and warmer, and Slimane needed to pull himself together, because next he had to discuss the Algerian War of Independence and the female voice in the work of Assia Djebar, whereas he was paying heed only to the discreet sensuality contained in the voice of the reader. There was also, of course, the issue of transmission in this novel, but he wasn't thinking of Mina, Zoulikha's daughter; his scholarly attention focused on relations between teacher and learner. He recalled the French officer Costa and the violence in the book, but the violence he was experiencing now consisted of maintaining his self-control while Noor was within reach of his hands and his bed, disturbingly confined. As a consequence, the constraints faced by the heroine in the novel became mixed up in his mind with a process of initiation, as a person might put her life as a young girl behind her. Like the author, he found himself striving to transcend such notions as desire: persistent desire, buried desire, revealed desire; violence, contained violence—he went over them ad infinitum. By this twisting path, he managed despite everything to catch hold of himself at the moment when Noor's voice was saying: *I had to get away from all that.* The young woman, moved, put the book back down in her lap and waited for comments from her teacher. The latter came back to earth, which is to say, found himself speechless before his student. To regain his composure a little, he fixed a smile on his lips.

"Very good."

He took some time. He too was moved, though not for the same reasons. He asked what else she had read of this novelist. She mentioned *Fantasia, A Sister to Scheherazade,* and *So Vast the Prison.* Noor remained as distant as ever and, at the same time, warmer than any woman. Slimane could not understand the sort of living oxymoron she was. They spoke a little, but not much, because Slimane felt himself in a fog, and the themes he'd wished to discuss with her had gradually faded away, overcome by his personal imagination. He felt disheartened. He kept thinking she was impassioned; then the next moment she went back to being cold as opal or sapphire or ruby. He no longer wished to linger in her company—it hurt too much. A dull, nagging pain was in fact taking root in the pit of his stomach. He needed to lie down and breathe calmly for a while. Later he'd see. Actually, it would be an excuse to have her come back more than once, till the day when . . .

"We have to finish now; I have some other meetings. We'll have much more to say. With Assia Djebar, one needs to go deep. Come at the same time, same day next week."

He got up and offered her his hand.

"You don't mind? Really?" She smiled. "It's kind of you."

Standing in front of him, the young woman returned his handshake for longer than normal, thought Slimane.

"Till next week," she said.

Slimane experienced the entire scene as a moment of extreme happiness, which made him awkward as he opened the door.

"See you again soon, Monsieur Slimane," she said as she walked down the few steps.

Sese and Ichrak—the latter had just arrived, and Mme Bouzid had disappeared—were doubled over laughing in the middle of the courtyard. After a final gesture, the young Congolese regained his composure and said, "So anyway, Ichrak, I puff out my chest, I put on this charismatic expression, and I say to the guy: 'Listen, pal! Do you know who I am?' The guy goes: 'Me, I'm Captain Mosisa Ekemba of the intelligence service. State your name, sir!' Shit, Ichrak! I had to wriggle out of it somehow if I didn't want to end up in solitary, beaten till I bled and tortured with a rusty screwdriver. So I say to him: 'I'm Sese Seko. Yes, I am!' Oh—Professor Slimane!" Sese turned toward the teacher. "How's it going, prof?"

Slimane Derwich did not like the familiarity with which Sese often treated him.

"Good morning," he grunted.

When Ichrak greeted him in turn, he didn't even answer but spun on his heel and returned to his room. Before closing the door, he saw Sese and the young woman heading to the street and laughing.

What do they get up to, those two, all those hours they spend together? I shouldn't even be wondering about it, Slimane Derwich thought to himself. Shutting herself away with that dog! Doing what? Even Saïda Bouzid forgets herself when she's talking to him. In the meantime, Noor's putting on airs and pushing me gradually to the limit. During the long while he'd spent with her, he'd been mostly present, but he felt he'd barely existed in the young woman's perception; she'd had no time for anyone except Assia Djebar and the veiled *Woman without Sepulcher* at her police station. To put it differently, he'd felt himself to be a sort of abstraction, an idea as it were, or something even vaguer.

5

CYCLONE

DRAMÉ AND SESE were sitting at a sidewalk table on Place des Nations Unies, having falafel and mint tea together. All the tables were occupied. The row of restaurants offered anything from shawarma to homemade couscous, from pizza to Thai food. The nearby streets were packed. Stores were selling everything the country had to offer in the way of craftsmanship and decorative objects. Wherever space permitted, itinerant sellers had spread their wares, displaying cell phone peripherals, all sorts of clothing, sunglasses, umbrellas. Teenagers accosted the passersby, hawking Orange or Inwi top-ups. There were plenty of places to get a quick meal, especially a dish of little snails served in a sauce that was to die for. Beggars, old women, or children made appeals to compassion. It didn't always work. But there were crowds of people, and some felt a sufficient pang of guilt that they handed over a few coins or a banknote—why not?

"Dramé, over there—check her out. What a figure; see how she moves. Lord."

"Cool down. Aren't you meeting with Ichrak?"

"Yeah, we have things to do. But Ichrak's a sister to me. Me, I need a *go*, a girl. I can't stay like this, with the chicks on my computer and nothing else. It doesn't work for me."

"And ogling like that does? You Congolese, you'll never change—you're too sentimental by half. What was it you were telling me the other day, something about *miso te*?"

"Kwanga ya moninga bityaka yango miso te—don't stare at someone else's cassava loaf."

"There you go. This is Islam here, my brother. Here you can't just gawk at women and chat with them the way you would in Rome or Paris. It's barely tolerated to talk to a woman at all. They can approach you, not the other way around. For me it's OK; I'm Baye Fall, a Senegalese Sufi. I have an excuse; women can't get enough of my dreads hanging down my back when I'm stripped to the waist, *wallah*! Hey, let me introduce you to someone who thinks like you, who likes it when they sway—a compatriot of yours, as it happens."

A guy was coming hesitantly toward them from the intersection. He gave the impression of walking on a cloud; his gaze was absent. He was wearing blue jeans, a New York Giants shirt, and babouche slippers. His shoulders were as broad as the Berlin Wall—he was a strapping fellow, no doubt about it. Yet he looked as if the slightest breeze would sweep him effortlessly away. It was as if his insides had been hollowed out and there was nothing left to help him keep his balance.

"I've been looking for you, Dramé," he said. "In the medina they told me you were eating around here. I just got a message from Doja. It's been a long time, dammit! Will you translate it for me?"

It was only then that he seemed to notice Sese.

"Oh! Afternoon, brother," he mumbled.

"It's cool," said Sese.

"Sese, this is Gino Katshinda, a Congolese from Kinshasa like yourself."

Sese studied the newcomer. The guy really wasn't in great shape. His speech was slurred and his eyes lifeless, as happens with people who take antipsychotic medication. His clothing was uncared for, a clear sign of self-neglect. And when that happens to a Congolese, who usually respects himself and lets the world know it, you don't need a psychiatrist to tell you that the neurons have gone AWOL. Gino held his smartphone out to Dramé. The latter seemed bothered; he lifted a tired hand to the phone, took it, focused on the screen, and read in silence.

"What does she say?" asked Gino in a hurried whisper, anxiously, as if his life depended on the answer.

Dramé didn't reply. Frowning, he read some more, then put the phone in sleep mode and handed it back.

"She says that everything is fine; her father's forgiven her now."

"That's all? It looked longer than that."

"She says that they're waiting for a government to be formed and that she hopes you'll see each other again. She also says she loves you, that she can't live without you."

"In any case, thank you, you're a brother to me," said Gino, putting his phone away.

He fumbled some more in his pockets, produced a pair of dark glasses in frames made up of little circles, and, as if Sese and Dramé had turned into some gaseous substance—were no longer there—he went back the way he'd come. A loud car horn sounded, and Gino stopped in his tracks as if by remote control; a streetcar, paying no attention to the small fry, continued on its course like a long, carefree snake, its carapace designed by computer. The gust from the vehicle made Gino tremble like a leaf. Once it passed, he continued unfazed across the tracks, seeming to float as he walked.

"The fuck is up with that brother? He's far gone!"

"Libya," said Dramé. "Before, he was full of energy. I saw him almost every day. We went there together. It's his girlfriend from there that writes to him. He came to see me so I could translate for him. Arabic's hard to read."

"But what did you tell him? He was right; it looked like you read much more than you said."

"Yeah, man, but it's a tough situation. Over a year ago we went there, him and me."

"To do what? Since Sarkozy stuck his oar in and killed Gaddafi, the place is messed up."

"When a place is messed up, there's money to be made."

"There's nothing there!"

"Sure there is. There are migrants. You see Gino there? He was a big name, I'm telling you. It wasn't that long ago people still called him the Mayor of Casa. He was a style maven. You'd never have caught him wearing slippers back then. He could make you any kind of document you wanted, certificates, you name it—I swear on my mother. The guy you just saw was a dab hand at embossed stamps and official signatures; he could put a microchip in a passport with one hand tied behind his back. In Libya they needed someone like that. Because with migrants, what do you sell them? Papers! We started in Ghat, near the Algerian border, but there wasn't much happening there. We had to go farther north, and we ended up in Murzuq. Fuck, man, you should have seen the place. Everyone's packing there, even the kids. From a young age, they're taught to hate Blacks, so you need to keep a low profile. There's nothing left there—no businesses, no work, no government—so Kalashnikovs make the law. Blacks aren't liked anywhere, but there even less than other places. So as to blend in and go unnoticed, we started looking for work. This one guy hired us to repaint his house and outbuildings. He was a businessman; it was good. Plus he put us up. The problem was that he had a daughter, Doja. The one that sent the message. Gino decided he was going to hit on her."

"Hit on her? In Libya? He's nuts, your pal."

"I told him as much! We had work, there were orders for papers and everything, money was coming in. I kept telling him every day: 'Don't even think about it.' But he said the girl was being more and more insistent. It was no good repeating to him that Islam in Libya wasn't easygoing; it wasn't like Senegal. If he started messing around, they'd kill the both of us and in really bad ways. It was like talking to a wall. He did it."

"Fuck me! He tried it on with her?"

"Worse—he took her virginity."

"What an idiot!"

"Damn right. He came to tell me, but he was totally stressed. He said that right afterward, at the moment when he was feeling all happy and relaxed, the kid ups and tells him she'll have to confess everything to her dad; otherwise, there'll be hell to pay on her marriage day. She couldn't keep it a secret; her father had to know. I mean, he was the boss of everything."

"What then?"

"It was late evening. I didn't wait around; I grabbed my stuff. I told Gino to do the same, the fuckwad, and we rushed off to look for a car to rent so we could hightail to the border. Before the father could lay his hands on us—because he was going to come after us. Once we made the frontier, it cost us the earth to cross to Algeria."

"So what did the message say, that one today?"

"It sucks, man. I could never let him know the truth. I've only told him that the father was furious and that he'd beaten the kid. I can't tell him that she's been confined to the house for more than a year, that she was pregnant by him; she must have given birth already, and now she has to live close to men, women, and children from all over Africa that are penned up in her father's courtyard like animals. You saw the state Gino's in after that business; he's filled with remorse. Here she writes that recently she's been waking up to the whine of machines cutting and soldering iron.

She's been moved from her room and put in another one that looks out onto the courtyard where her father's building cages, man. I've got friends who passed through Libya—Gambians, Nigerians, Eritreans—and they told me the people were catching migrants in the desert. You've no idea where you are out there, but those people know the place well. They keep them as hostages till someone forks out a ransom through Western Union from Gao or Kidal or Mogadishu. They had to pay fourteen thousand dinars— a hundred fifty euros—several times over before they reached the border. Sometimes there are these strange shouts, even gunshots. Night or day. They bury the bodies right there."

"Everyone knows what it's like over there . . . Gino's already gone weird because of the girl. It's just as well he doesn't know everything."

"He's traumatized, man."

"He should've been traumatized when the kid came on to him. He'd be in a lot better shape today."

At this moment Sese spotted a familiar figure: Ichrak, from a distance, was gesturing to him to hurry up and pointing to a streetcar that was approaching at high speed and heading in the direction of Boulevard Mohammed V.

"I gotta go, buddy. I have some business with the girl."

"Tell her hello from me."

Sese tossed a couple of banknotes on the table and ran for the streetcar.

"Hey, Sese, what's the point of your Nikes if you can't run as fast as Michael Jordan?" Ichrak teased him. "Is Mme Bouzid feeding you too well?"

"You expect me to arrive in front of you all out of breath? Charisma above all."

With a sort of bow, he gestured toward the door of the streetcar as she opened it.

"After you, dear girl."

The door sighed as it closed. Then there was a soft sliding noise; the fifty tons of Alstom Citadis machinery trembled, but very gently, thanks to its 750-kilowatt engine and 720 volts of tension. The panoramic windows showed palm trees, the tower of the medina, the Hyatt Regency, the highest floors of the BCMI Bank building. The sun had begun its downward course, and the sky had acquired an orange tinge. At the intersection with Place des Nations Unies, accelerating cars were releasing clouds of exhaust fumes, the drivers leaning on the horn to clear a safe passage. Headlights were already turned on. On the sidewalks, vendors of desert water, dressed in their traditional red costumes and tall conical hats, were trying to sell their last drop of liquid, served from a tin bowl that caught the last sparse rays. Nearby, shopkeepers were feverishly busy before the final whistle. Passersby were hurrying home. The bus stops were crowded with people exhausted after a hard day of work, while, in the saffron-colored light, the voice of the muezzin soared majestically, a sure comfort in the face of the challenges that arose every day with the dawn when it appeared over Casablanca, the city also known as Ad-dar Al Baidaa'.

⁓

It had taken some time before Ichrak joined Sese in business. She was known to be cautious. Not wanting to prove her reputation wrong, she'd held back before following through on her promise, but in the end she'd paid a visit to the young Congolese. His room was sparsely furnished: a bed, curtains, a work surface with his computer in pride of place, two chairs, and a soft armchair in the corner. The two of them were sitting side by side in front of the screen. Ichrak was staring at it with an expression of distrust mingled with disdain, so as to hide her discomfort with the test that awaited her, even though she'd warned Sese that showing anything at all was out of the question. Ichrak was hoping that Sese was right and that her beauty would do all the work, though she had her doubts. When a three-toned signal sounded, the two of them sat up. A face appeared. The guy looked like President Hollande, but with bags under the eyes, graying hair, and an entirely different haircut. His name was in fact François.

"Hello?" he said.

Sese was sitting out of view of the camera, like a prompter in the theater.

"Show him your smile," he whispered to Ichrak.

"Good morning," she said, smiling.

Sese could tell it was already in the bag. Ichrak's smile and a few "ahs" and "ohs" she uttered, followed by a sigh, after every second or third sentence spoken by the mark, had already put the latter in an indescribable condition. He clearly wanted only one thing now: to jump through the screen and throw his arms around this woman who was smiling with such warmth and conviction. After a few minutes of chat—"Where do you live?"; "What do you do?"; "Are you married, François?"—supplemented by various facial expressions at Sese's cuing, the latter whispered: "Lean forward, go on!"

The young woman had brought three different traditional outfits, and Sese had gauged the amount of cleavage she should show. He knew the internet: it shouldn't be too deep or too little; it just needed to cause an electric shock. The simple act of imagining Ichrak's chest—Sese could attest to this himself—was already a journey in itself. When the young woman moved even closer to the tiny LED lamp above the screen, a solemn silence ensued, in which nothing could be heard except the humming of the computer's occasionally creaky fan, whose cogs also seemed to have been knocked sideways. From time to time, Ichrak uttered a murmur as soft as a faint breeze at the start of the rainy season, or an "ah . . ." followed by a slight outbreath that came from deep within. On the other side of the screen, some crucial thing was palpably about to take place. Sese didn't want to look, but he saw a shadow moving regularly and at increasing speed.

"The screenshot!" he whispered.

It was probably a little too loud, but the guy no longer heard anything and wasn't seeing much either. Ichrak clicked on SnapMyScreen.

"You can sign off."

"François?"

No reply, just the rubbing of fabric.

"I have to go," said Ichrak.

"Wait!" begged François, on the verge of apoplexy.

That was the moment she chose to break off the conversation.

"Excellent!"

The two of them high-fived.

"You see, it's easy. Because you cut it off like that, deliberately, he'll contact you again. Not now. He's seen you; the rest will follow of its own accord—don't you worry about that. You'll have another session; then one evening I'll appear and tell him what's what, after I've gone online and tracked down his wife and kids, his friends and coworkers. I'll make him fork out—he's a regular guy; he'll be scared. You saw him, right?"

"You're nuts, Sese. Poor man."

"He'll only get what he deserves. What is it with these people and their weird habits? Plus, admiring your cleavage, just like that? For nothing? Surely you're joking, my sister."

"Whereas you, my brother, you're not joking at all."

"Obviously."

That day, the fellow called François was not the only victim of Ichrak's irresistible attraction.

Just before she and Sese arrived in front of the Café Jdid, Si Miloud was watching his game but pretending not to, counting on a mistake by Abdelwahed, who, in turn, was swearing at what he saw in his hand while at the same time—and for the same reason—cursing all his playing companions together. Ramdam was drinking whey. He was mentally thanking his mother—may God mind her soul—for having conceived such an intelligent son, because every card he'd put down had been well played. At the moment when Mekloufi was about to take everyone down by playing a suit that no one expected, he broke off his turn in midgesture, hand in the air, because Ichrak and Sese came into view. The young woman had gathered her hair together, and a stray strand drifted over her right eye, adding mystery to her features and stirring the emotions of the card players. Plus, she was wearing an electric-blue dress with thin straps, loose fitting at the waist and reaching down almost to her knees. The leather thongs of her flat sandals looped around her ankles, emphasizing their curve. The young people were still twenty yards away, yet the four customers sitting on the terrace were already salivating. Taken by surprise, their nervous systems were now transmitting impulses only to the middle of their bodies, toward the stomach and what lay below.

When Sese greeted them with a "salaam alaikum," none of them dared to listen to the discreet greeting in Ichrak's imposing, velvety voice, for fear of damnation. Mekloufi alone, thanks to his past life as a hashish trafficker, was able to maintain a little sangfroid and respond with something more or less appropriate, but the raised hand, intended to triumph, fell back onto the table. He could only shake his head in resignation, because the woman's walk as she passed close by, and one glance too many at her fabulous hips, had utterly overwhelmed the players' metabolism, plunging it into low-battery mode in which it could consume only minimal energy. They all suddenly felt tired, their brains veering away so as to escape this purely animal attraction. The poor wretches couldn't help themselves. With Ichrak, everything was just a little bit too much, though it was a "too much" that called to mind an abundance brought under control, a frenzied lavishness, a generosity that brought relief. The steatopygic vision, beneath a wasplike waist, worked with complete diabolical precision, like one of those celestial spheres that constitute planets in the vast starry firmament and tower over us so magnificently. They were deeply moved, and Mekloufi's eagerly anticipated victory no longer counted for anything. Struck as he was, the former trafficker preferred to breathe and to meditate for a moment before felling his adversaries, who were still befuddled, paralyzed with emotion, their gaze fixed on an imaginary horizon of arabesques forming the suprapoetic morphology of that sublime apparition.

⁓

Sitting on a bench topped with a thin mattress, Ichrak was watching an ant as it crossed the wall in front of her, carrying something that looked like a grain of semolina. She'd been wondering how the insect had managed to find sustenance in a place that breathed such destitution. Her heart was pounding, and she'd been overcome with worry ever since the police car driven by Lahcen Choukri had intercepted her at the corner of Boukra and Moulay-Youssef. She still didn't understand what had happened.

That afternoon, while she was out, her mother had thrown away a week's supply of pills in one of her fits of madness, then had told Ichrak she didn't want to take them anymore because someone had poisoned them. In the evening her mental state had deteriorated. It had seemed to Ichrak that her mother's brain was about to burst—she'd shouted endless curses and threats against the whole world, but especially aimed at Ichrak herself. The young woman had had to leave in the middle of the night to get medication from a pharmacist she knew. It was on her way back home that she'd run into Choukri. She was in danger of being detained till the morning; meanwhile, her mother was alone, prey to her demons and their torments. She had to leave. But no one had come to see her; she hadn't even been questioned.

When Daoudi entered the station and saw how pleased Choukri was to see him, he felt at once there must be something in it for him. Had the young officer captured public enemy number one? No way. In Derb Taliane the competition for that title was too great. Had some jihadist recruiter been unmasked? If that had been the case, such a person would long ago have been torn to pieces in the neighborhood. The young detective had always admired Daoudi, and he wanted to emulate him in certain character traits, particularly his way of acting cool, like his other idol, Booba. He liked the firmness Daoudi showed toward his team. But he also sensed a thoroughly paternal kindness toward himself, to the point that he wanted to please his chief whenever he could. Before Choukri could even open his mouth, Daoudi said, "Out with it. What it is you want to tell me?"

"You'll never guess, sir."

"Did I win the lottery?"

"Almost, sir—and it's thanks to my vigilance. She's here."

"Who's here?"

"Ichrak. She's waiting for you."

"Where?"

"In a cell, of course—where do you think? You told me that if I ever see her, I should bring her in for you. So I did."

A glint appeared in Daoudi's eye.

"Do you know why I gave you that mission?" he asked. "Because I have confidence in you. I knew that you were the only one who could carry it off. You're better than a son. Never would a son have offered his father what you're bringing me today. Never, you hear?"

The inspector went into his office, not without conceding a smile that quickly hardened, to show that self-possession of his. The younger detective was too emotional to speak. All his feelings were expressed in snapping to attention, his hand on the visor of his cap with its OKLM badge.

Lahcen Choukri liked to drive around in the evening, the powerful bass of his stereo pulsing through the open windows. On Boulevard Moulay Youcef, heading toward the sea, for a few miles he'd felt like Dr. Dre on Main Street, Compton. Booba's solemn voice murmured from the baffles: "Street life, ain't no diplomatic immunity / I'm there to fuck everything, not to save humanity." The street—or *la rue*, as they said on the outskirts of Paris and in Casa—was Lahcen Choukri's reason for living. It was for that that he'd opted for a career in law and order. At school he'd read *Zaman Al-Akhtaâ aw Al-Shouttar—Time of Mistakes*—the magnificent novel by Mohamed Choukri, and it had left a lasting impression on him. From that moment he knew how a thief, a killer, a whore, thought and operated. He was so taken with the author that he started an urban legend according to which Mohamed Choukri was none other than his own uncle—brother of his father and a former crook—and that he'd written the book for him, his nephew Lahcen, so he'd stay on the straight and narrow. Choukri did such a good job of convincing everyone else that he ended up believing his own lie. The street, mediated by literature, became a true school for him. Later on, reading not being his strong suit, he made do with the wisdom of the Senegalese rapper Booba, who knew almost as much about the subject as his uncle, while Booba's sentences were a lot shorter and easier to memorize. His "metagores" ripped into you like nothing else, and the guy had outfits and a look that inspired Lahcen even more. He was just thinking about getting his whole forearm tattooed when he caught sight of a figure he recognized on the sidewalk. He quickly double-parked, put his flashing light on the dashboard, and got out of the car. He went swiftly up to Ichrak, grabbed her by the arm, and, opening the passenger side door, said, "Get in!"

She fought back. "What do you want!" she shouted.

"No talking!"

Flashes of blue lit up the beautiful woman's face. With a powerful hand, Choukri pushed her into the front seat and slammed the door. Ichrak tugged at the door handle, but it couldn't be opened from inside. Choukri cuffed her and set off toward the station. Ichrak yelled insults in the young cop's ears while Booba was coming right out with it: "La rue made me crazy, I'm crazy about her / I only have eyes for her / She's the only one for me / I've fallen for her." Lahcen showed only indifference and cool, like his two mentors, one of whom was singing right now, to bass frequencies and snare drum. The singer added, as if warning the girl, "Not a fucking thing to be done, you say the wrong thing you're asswipe / I don't wanna make peace but lemme smoke the peace pipe." Lahcen Choukri resembled his idol: he was the hunter, never the prey, and he liked the feeling it gave him.

An infinity passed before the cell door opened. Daoudi had waited for the station to empty before going to see the young woman. Ichrak started in surprise when she recognized the inspector.

Up till now their relationship had not exactly been cordial. After their first encounter, they'd crossed paths two or three times. One day, he'd offered her a lift, but things had not gone well. Daoudi had thought he was all set. He stopped the Dacia in a side street off Boulevard de la Corniche where there was construction. The broad blue ocean glinted in the distance, but for Daoudi it was only a backdrop that played no part in his decision. He didn't beat about the bush. To him, a girl who accepted a second ride in a car knew what she wanted. The moment the engine was turned off and the parking brake applied, he took her hand. He made as if he was going to stroke it, but he put it on his erection. Ichrak jumped as if she'd touched a snake, and she grabbed his wrist. Then she lunged for the door.

"What's wrong with you?" Daoudi barked.

"Is all the sea not enough for you?" Ichrak replied, waving her arm in that direction. "What more do you want?"

"You!"

"And this is how you plan to go about it?"

"You slut! Why did you get in the car?"

Ichrak opened the door, got out, and strode off toward the boulevard in search of a cab. She swore to herself that from now on she'd keep her distance from this cop.

"So my men also took you for a whore?"

His body dominated the cramped space of the cell.

"Let me out, Mokhtar; you know me."

"You're questioning Choukri's competence? He's my best guy. He knows how to spot girls like you. He saw you walking down that sidewalk."

The inspector was watching the young woman, eyes narrowed, like a cat weighing up the chances of a mouse that's strayed where it shouldn't have. Ichrak was on the verge of panic.

"I was on my way home; I'd gone to get medication for my mother." She rummaged in her handbag and took out a small box of pills, but Daoudi didn't even glance at it. "Please, Mokhtar."

"Remember how you behaved the last time we saw each other?"

"Let me out."

"Let you out? Only mountains never meet up. Now you're here, surely you don't think things are going to happen like the last time? You know, in the desert, always be the one that has the water and the camel. I have both, and you have nothing."

Ichrak's brain was spinning, but no solution came to mind. She absolutely had to get out of this hole. Her mother couldn't be left alone all night; anything could happen.

Daoudi went on: "I know you don't walk the streets; you'd never do that. I ought to let you go, but here honey, you're going to be a whore for me."

He walked up to her where she sat on a filthy mattress in this tiny cell in the police station on Rue Souss, in the working-class neighborhood known as Cuba, like the Cuba all the way across the ocean.

~

As an alpha male, Saqr Al-Jasser had found it a good omen that the part of town open to the ocean bore the sweet name of Ain Diab, or Wolf Spring. It was here that the Saudi millionaire had gone to work, carrying out his first acquisitions of property as part of a three-phase operation that he planned to repeat: evict, demolish, build luxury housing. Buoyed by his initial success, he was intending to follow exactly the same MO in the natural continuation of this area: the neighborhoods of Derb Taliane and Cuba. The nabob had decided to turn these places into a private, exclusive site where only wolves would be allowed to drink the water. That animal being what it is and knowing only one way of proceeding, he had decided to follow his natural instinct and put himself in hunt mode, choosing as his number two the lovely and wealthy Farida Azzouz. If the wolf had set his heart on Farida, that too was not a matter of chance: in her he had recognized another of his kind. In fact, in each pack there exists an alpha female, and Farida fitted the role to a T. But you couldn't have everything. She was much too independent for Al-Jasser's liking.

So he settled for champing at the bit. Still, he applauded after the closing note from a singer accompanied by a trio on a stage in the center of the room. The musicians were a perfect match for the Moorish decor of Rick's Café, comprising a balcony, a gallery, and arches, all dotted with greenery to add freshness and provide moving shadows. It was a pleasant locale that closely resembled the movie *Casablanca*, as it was meant to, drawing busloads of tourists from Japan, China, America. It had been a stroke of genius by whoever had created the restaurant. The intrigue involving Humphrey Bogart as a spy could never have taken place in this city, though: the hotbed of espionage had been Tangiers, a less marketable name than Casablanca, the "white house." There had indeed been arches and potted plants in the Rick's Café of the film, but here, for the visitors they were much more real, like those Mickey Mouses and Daisy Ducks handing out leaflets at Disneyland—they acknowledge you; you can take selfies with them; they're not made of pasteboard. So people descend en masse upon this dream arising from another dream, believing that they're drinking from the same whiskey glass as Bogie when he sees Ingrid Bergman enter his bar and declares with a melancholy look on his face, "Of all the gin joints in all the towns, in all the world, she walks into mine." This whole reality was fake, and no one cared; they were only waiting for one thing, to hear, "Play it again, Sam," uttered by one of the waiters to the musicians of the "oriental" band, even if one of them was actually called Samir. Al-Jasser knew how profitable a well-exploited concept could be. He was counting on doing the same in building futuristic infrastructures upon the ruins of Derb Taliane and Cuba: a five-star hotel, a huge shopping mall with luxury stores glittering like gold riyals, a pedestrian zone paved like the streets of paradise, a tunnel under Avenue Tiznit with giant aquarium walls to make it seem like you're under the sea, fountains with crystalline waters wherever you look, benches where families can rest a while like in an ad for happiness. The present decor was perfect for the conversation he was about to have with Farida Azzouz—that too would have its fake elements and its convolutions, like the voice of the singer at that moment.

The music had started up again, and a lament led Saqr Al-Jasser's thoughts away from business matters, to the diners whispering to one another as they ate. He observed the play of shadow and light on the wall hangings and the canvas canopy over the terrace. It was a moment of respite before his interview with the lady. He didn't like feeling attracted to her. For a moment, despite himself, as he gazed at the backlit space, his mind was drawn to the smooth inside of Farida Azzouz's knees, revealed in brief glimpses by the silk of her dress. It was the kind of occurrence that hindered him from negotiating properly, which is to say, remaining firm. And he was at this very moment bending to her will: he'd been waiting for her for more than twenty minutes. It had been the same story the last time they met. That was what he didn't like about this country: their Islam wasn't strict enough. The women permitted themselves all kinds of things. Where he was from, he wouldn't even have had to talk to her. Morocco still had a long way to go in the management of women.

True, Mme Azzouz had the upper hand. He needed the land cleared of those damned apartment buildings that did nothing but spoil the view. To complete his investment, he only had to secure those few hundred square yards. And this bitch was claiming that she first needed to have people evicted. Admittedly that wasn't an easy matter. Some of the apartments were occupied by hard-core locals, families that had been there for generations, like the Azzouzes. Others had been vacated when the price was right, but very quickly, nature abhorring a vacuum, they'd been squatted in by migrants, leaving no apartment free. These people—men, women, children—were from all sorts of different countries to the south. At this point, Farida had had to resort to hired men to try and collect on at least some of the rents. In a universe obeying no laws, with a population that had braved the merciless desert and was prepared to risk the ocean and the storm, nothing less than a rent collector as wily as Guerrouj was called for.

The laws in this country are badly made, Saqr was thinking as he checked his watch. He was about to curse to himself, but something got in the way: a cloud of scent suddenly disturbed the course of his musings. Farida had just made her appearance. She was dazzling, in a black Yves Saint Laurent gown and Manolo Blahnik pumps. A Cartier Panthère yellow gold bracelet set flames dancing on her forearm. She sat down opposite Saqr. Before she'd finished crossing her legs, her hands had crossed the table and come to rest on one of his wrists, each finger moving separately on his skin. Saqr loathed that habit of hers of being so tactile. It stopped him from concentrating.

"How are you, my dear friend? I'm sorry for being late, but you know how it is in business. I said to myself, 'Mr. Al-Jasser must be so angry at me; I always make him wait.' But you don't hold it against me, I'm certain of it," she added, emphasizing the point by stroking him with her fingernails.

Saqr made an effort to prevent the short-circuit that was being triggered in his head, and managed to regain his impartiality, as far as his senses were concerned, that is. The arrival of the waiter had helped.

"What can I bring you, ma'am?"

"A Laszlo daiquiri, heavy on the rum."

"Another Jack Daniel's for me."

The waiter disappeared. Saqr complimented his companion's choice. He had this accursed business to settle, and he was also hoping to get her into bed. But first, the discussion needed to be brought to a conclusion.

"My dear Farida, how could I possibly hold anything against you when you've merely prolonged the pleasure?" As banter went it was a bit of a cliché, but Saqr hadn't yet fully recovered from Farida's triumphal entry. "Tell me, though—where do we stand with our negotiations? When are we going to be able to sign?"

"I'm working hard on it. I'm almost there. Soon I'll have the necessary permits, and I'll be able to evict all those people. You have no idea how they're poisoning my life. It's costing me a fortune. But what can I do? Hospitality is one of the pillars of Islam, is it not?"

Saqr was aghast at such bad faith. She was playing for time, speaking of the migrants, when all that was needed was a flamethrower and the job would be over. She was going to haggle over the price; that much was sure. And he was pressed for time. The consortium he worked for had given him an ultimatum. They drew the line at a loan that had been followed by a whole year of negotiations. Furthermore, the banks had demanded a considerable contribution from his own funds, and they would only sign off when they saw a document certifying the sale of the land. Up to that point his money was tied up, and so far the only security Farida Azzouz had offered him had been her word. She was stalling far too much, and with the increasing delays, he had little hope of finalizing everything in time. Something stank. Could there be a competitor? After doing some digging, Saqr had learned that apparently one of Farida's reasons for jacking up the price was because she was up to her neck in mortgages. She would do anything to get what she wanted.

The waiter brought their drinks.

"You know, Saqr, I want to please you," said Farida after taking a long sip through a straw. She put her glass back down. "That's always been my desire, and you know it. I promise you: just a few more weeks, and we'll have moved forward. I'm working on it all the time."

Saqr Al-Jasser studied his interlocutor, wondering if she was being sincere. He lingered over her features, looking for the lie, but this clouded his judgment since, in the subdued lighting, he saw only a flawless visage. She continued to speak—about property law, about difficulties in the area of investments, about what was at stake for the future. As he listened, Saqr watched her index finger, which was holding the straw in her glass upright and moving it in a circular motion. Meanwhile the throaty-voiced singer was detailing the torments her lover subjected her to day after day. With her every gesture, her every glance, Farida contrived to weave an invisible web around her companion. It was all about reducing the scope of his reflections and bringing him back to terrain that she controlled, so she could then manipulate him at will. With more sips of alcohol, the heady music, and the Hollywood atmosphere, the result was not long in coming: the Saudi was only half listening, his mind on other things now.

"What would you say to continuing this conversation in my suite? I'm right next door, in the Sofitel. I'll have a bottle of champagne sent up. I want to see the stars shining in your eyes."

Farida seemed lost for words, then regarded Al-Jasser with a gaze of immense tenderness. She took his hand in both of hers.

"Goodness, I had no idea you were so . . . so altruistic! How did you know?"

"Know what?"

"You're a mind reader, Saqr. For my husband!"

"I'm sorry?"

"That's exactly what he said to me the first time he invited me to drink champagne with him at his place: 'I want to see the stars shine in your eyes.' I'd forgotten it, but you reminded me, right here, today. Thank you. You can't imagine how touched I am."

Spontaneously, she waxed lyrical on the admiration she felt for her husband, who was so elegant in the way he thought, in his opinions, in everything he undertook, especially in the area of theater and the arts. It went on for ten minutes at least. Right afterward, she returned to her apartment buildings and the poor

Africans who had fled war only to find themselves at the mercy of human traffickers, braving the desert and the sun, then finally finding refuge with her, Farida Azzouz. But at the same time, they messed up the plumbing, damaged the walls, were always late with their rent. She kept up about that for another quarter of an hour or so, then moved on to her duties as a Muslim—which she mustn't ever lose sight of. She even brought in two or three suras on hospitality as points of reference, each one accompanied by a caress on Saqr's forearm with her middle finger.

After half an hour or more of this treatment, Al-Jasser lost the thread, and his eyes began straying around the restaurant. Then, for lack of the smooth insides of Farida Azzouz's knees, he started thinking about the three elegantly dressed, unaccompanied young women he'd seen sitting at the bar in the Sofitel. His thoughts lingered over the one who wore her hair in a chignon that brought out the delicacy in the nape of her neck. He wondered when his guest was going to stop talking, hoping she'd go, so he could finally satisfy his appetite for flesh. Wolves understand one another through facial expressions, posture, little moans, smells—including Givenchy or Dior. Saqr had this down, but Farida seemed to be disturbing the code. Her face gave the impression of desire, but her words expressed something else entirely. Al-Jasser was unsettled, and he had no wish to lose his appetite. He was hungry. The wolf devours its prey in its entirety, bones and skin included. With Farida things were not going particularly well, so he concentrated his ambitions on one of the gazelles from the hotel bar—she at least was there to satisfy voracious men like himself. She would pretend to be eaten in full; you just had to ask the price.

～

Ichrak and Sese had become virtually inseparable. The young woman liked his company, and in Derb Taliane and Cuba, people had grown used to their partnership. Ichrak had gained if not a brother, then a friend she could count on. After delivering batches of paper sacks to various stores, they had made their way through the crowd thronging the narrow streets and galleries of the medina.

Here you could find prêt-à-porter from Gucci, Armani, Hilfiger, and Dolce & Gabbana, as well as Adidas, Puma, and Nike Air shoes, all of which came from close by, from factories on the outskirts of the city. There were also smartphones of every type: top-of-the-line Apples were arranged in glass cases whose only security system was the eye of the stallholder, who sat on a stool nearby. Then there was leather, traditional clothing, expensive rugs woven from wool or from vegetable fibers if they were made in the Berber fashion. The shops selling argan oil looked like the ingot-filled interiors of bank vaults on Zurich's Bahnhofstrasse. The precious bottles of golden liquid, neatly lined up, covered the entire wall space; each boasted an official certificate bearing the kingdom's stamp, guaranteeing the source and nipping any haggling in the bud. The word *Kitoko*—"beauty," in Lingala— appeared in large letters across the facade of a small shop run by a local who spoke the language. A few yards away, a wide area was given over to merchants from various countries in Africa. Male and female hairdressers plied their trade on every corner; braids were plaited and unplaited by nimble female fingers, to the accompaniment of conversations shared by all those around. Aspiring young lookers tested their patience beneath the electric razor, finding distraction in the heavy syncopated bass of a Nigerian hit song. Here you could find *ndolé* just as easily as plantain, smoked fish as often as okra. People spoke languages from the center, the west, even the east of Ifriqiya. Every couple of steps an Ivorian, a Senegalese, or a Mauritanian called out to Sese with a "How's it going, Congo?" or "How are you, big man?" (when the speaker was younger) or "Your girlfriend's too good looking, Sese!" Ichrak was dressed simply in a black-and-white

Adidas tracksuit top with matching Converse high tops and a denim skirt, but her fluid, confident walk made all the difference, and the brothers could see it.

They entered the maze of alleyways, reached the bottom of Rue Goulmima, and turned onto it. Soon they crossed the arcades. The apartment building where Dramé lived was rather striking, even if the paint was faded and peeling. They opened the door without asking, then found themselves jostled in the doorway by Gino, who pushed past them, black rings under his eyes. He walked away without so much as a glance—it was like he was blind. He vanished from sight like a puff of smoke, car horns sounding to indicate his passage across the road.

"You see that guy? He messed up big time," Sese said to Ichrak. "Look what's happened to him. He's like a zombie, I swear."

"Messed up how?"

"I'll tell you later; it's a long story. There's a woman in Libya, a kid too I think."

In the stairwell they heard voices speaking Wolof and Bambara, Malinké and Fula.

"Follow me," said Sese.

They took the stairs to the third floor. Sese knocked at a door. It opened, and a face appeared framed in dreadlocks more than three or four fingers thick.

"Oh, Sese!" said Dramé, the Baye Fall, stepping back. "Come in, my brother!"

Sese let Ichrak enter first. They found themselves in a living room of about three hundred square feet, where two mattresses lying on rugs took up the entire space. Two guys were sitting there.

"I'm Abdoulaye," said one of them.

"Salaam alaikum!" the other said simply in greeting.

"The King of Congo is here! The Queen of Africa is present! Make room for them! Sit yourselves down; I'll be right there."

Their host headed for the kitchen, from where there came the smell of cooking.

"I'll just stir the sauce a bit and come back through. You have to keep an eye on *mafé*, or the peanuts can get burned."

Ichrak and Sese sat down. The only things on the almost bare walls were a framed verse from the Koran, a poster of Bob Marley with a joint in his mouth, and some clothes hanging on nails. On the ground in a corner was a pile of large PVC bags printed in blue or pink plaid patterns.

"How's it going, Sese? How are things at home?"

"Not bad."

"And your health?"

"Tip-top."

"*Alhamdulillah*—praise be to God. How's Lahla Saïda?"

"She's doing great."

"Alhamdulillah. What about the children?"

"They're really good."

"Alhamdulillah. And you, miss, how are you?"

"Very well, thank you," replied Ichrak.

"Your family's well?"

"Yes, thank you."

"Your health is good?"

"Alhamdulillah."

"Alhamdulillah."

"Ichrak, this is my buddy Dramé. Dramé taught me everything here. He's part of me; I'm part of him."

"He's exaggerating. He had talent; that's all there is to it. He's a Congolese; those guys know how to talk to women. Your presence here proves it. You're very beautiful, miss."

"Thank you."

"Don't pay any attention to him. This guy here is the grand priest of finance. He was trained by Nigerian cyberswindlers and Congolese *chekouleurs* who deal in fake certified checks.

He's all about bank transfers, emptying out accounts—he's a magician of secret codes, of fakery and its uses. He's got money rolling in. He's my mentor."

"Business isn't bad, but this part of the neighborhood isn't safe anymore, Sese. We get regular visits from guys threatening us. We can't take it much longer."

"The last time," Abdoulaye put in, "there were a dozen of them armed with iron rods and knives. They set fire to an apartment two buildings away."

"We're frightened now. If it keeps up, we'll have to leave here. That's what they want, man."

"Things will quiet down," Sese said, trying to reassure them.

"Quiet down? How? Near Tangiers a few years ago, at Boukhalef, they killed three Africans. They even slit the throat of a Senegalese guy from my neighborhood in Dakar."

"They killed him for nothing, my brother, nothing at all," lamented Abdoulaye, who had left Casamance and his native Ziguinchor simply to seek a little well-being elsewhere in the world.

"Boukhalef is the back of beyond. This is Casablanca, megapolis, the cosmopolitan world, my friend."

"Are you kidding, Sese? When it happens, there are agitators who put ideas in our own neighbors' heads about bumping us off, man. You see that group on the sidewalk opposite? They're troublemakers. They're like jackals, looking for small prey. Those guys are gonna lynch us one of these days. Come take a look."

Sese got up and crossed to the window. Half a dozen individuals were squatting along the arcades that lined the part of the street occupied by people selling newspapers, books, cigarettes, drinks. The men were stationed there to keep an eye on the apartment building and to do so as conspicuously as possible; at present, they were exchanging handshakes and laughing at something one of them had said. Sese quickly went back to the mattress.

"They're dangerous, man," Dramé went on. "They're never without a knife in their pocket. The last time, I got into it with one of them. Luckily there was a few of us. They're stirrers. In a situation like this, you need to be really careful."

"Really," said Abdoulaye.

The other guy sitting on the mattress wasn't saying a word, as if there was nothing to add—it was all inevitable.

Ichrak listened to the conversation with a heavy heart. It wasn't easy for any of them.

"It's true that there are problems here," she put in. "There are these rich people who want to kick folks out and put up apartment buildings and luxury stores from the seafront all the way into the neighborhood, but without us residents. Everyone's on edge, so it's enough for a few people to get upset; then the crowd takes it out on the first person to come along. It wasn't like that before. It was quiet here."

"Yet the government is planning to legalize over a hundred thousand African nationals," said Sese. "Have you ever heard of anything like that anywhere in the world? Slap bang in the middle of all this migration! When walls are going up all over the place."

"Those guys opposite are idiots. They don't get it! But there'll always be people like them. Plus, like my sister says, it's also a matter of dough, as always." Dramé got up. "I'm going to check on the mafé; that's much more interesting."

"Scootch over; it's hot!"

Dramé was coming back from the kitchen with a large serving dish heaped with rice and vegetables, topped with peanut sauce and accompanied with chunks of lamb. He put the food down on the rug and invited his guests to dig in.

"Everyone needs to eat! Ichrak, my sister, help yourself; it's good!"

Everyone leaned over the dish and began to eat, using their hands. Abdoulaye's friend still wasn't talking, merely biting into a piece of meat made tender by Dramé's magic.

"I ran into Gino downstairs as I was coming in," said Sese between mouthfuls. "Things are not going well for him. He looks completely out of it. Was he here?"

"Yeah, man. He had me read another of those messages. He can't get that girl out of his fucking head. It's bad. Over there anyone who has the space—a barn, some land, whatever—they kidnap migrants and confine them. Doja's father is showing her what he would have done to Gino if he'd caught him. Now he's started selling them like cattle out in the courtyard. It's African slavery all over again, man. The kid sees it almost every day; she can't take it any longer."

"Fuck!" was all Sese could say.

"Recently she's also seen Arabs in the cages, Moroccans or Tunisians. She doesn't get what's going on."

"God!" exclaimed Ichrak. "What are they going to do with them? Surely not sell them as slaves?"

"Who knows?"

"Didn't you say there was a child as well, Sese?"

"Dramé, that's enough about Gino. We're eating."

The aroma rising from the dish was delicious, but the conversation died down. After a few more mouthfuls, no one's heart was in it anymore, and Dramé cleared away the dishes. Sese and Ichrak left soon after, thanking their host for the meal. They walked downstairs without a word.

⌒

Like Dramé and Abdoulaye, though for different reasons, Sese had often thought about fleeing his native country, Congo, where he couldn't see a future for himself, what with the coltan ore and oil being discovered and the way the opposition was behaving. He wanted to go where people enjoyed the benefits of these materials, but he never came up with a plan. Yet as he entered the cabin of the Airbus 300 that was to take him to Lomé, he'd experienced it as the beginning of a longer journey. He'd been sent by his aunt Mujinga of Mbuji-Mayi to finalize the purchase of a consignment of pagnes. He'd been provided with three thousand dollars, part of which he'd exchanged for CFA francs. Once he arrived in the Togolese capital, he found his hotel. The next day, he was to go to the address he'd been given for the purchase, but as he passed through the Grand Market, he'd stopped in front of a table bearing essential charms: for seducing any woman you want, for blocking the effects of bad karma, for detecting someone who has a more powerful *grigri*, for passing a crucial university exam or signing an employment contract—in a word, there were numerous options. His attention was drawn to a bauble that was supposed to bring good luck by making you more alert. He didn't feel the pickpocket, who used a razorblade to slice open the small sack he was wearing across his shoulder. The thief managed to relieve him of a significant portion of his money. It was only when he wanted to pay for the amulet that he noticed what had happened.

"My money!" he shouted. "My money's been stolen!"

"Listen, my brother, you have to be quick!" said the stallholder in a drawling accent. He was a skinny guy with cheeks marked with tribal scarifications. "See," he added, pointing to a hairy object, "here I've got a monkey's finger that's specially treated so it can instantly identify the thief who wronged you. If you'd bought it five minutes ago, this would never have happened."

Sese stared ahead, forgot the amulets and the smooth talker, and plunged into the crowd in front of him as if he might recognize his own banknotes changing hands somewhere. Frantic, he wandered here and there until the sun rose too high, forcing him to seek shade in a sort of *malewa*, or unlicensed restaurant.

After he'd eaten something and drunk a soda, he started thinking. Going back to Kinshasa empty-handed was out of the question. His aunt would have a fit. But how could he find money, here, in a foreign country? It was a huge sum, which had been saved up over a long time. As he imagined going back south toward Congo, he thought to himself that if he headed north, it would be easier to come up with something and pay back Aunt Mujinga. In fact, he'd already completed a good part of the journey. He started thinking about the rest, about crossing West Africa, going as far north as possible. After that, why not, the ocean went all the way to Europe—to Spain, the crappiest of its countries. Yet even Spain was overflowing with euros, Sese was sure of it, let alone the Bundesrepublik, Sweden, the heights of Monaco or Marseille.

He paid for his food and left the little restaurant, telling himself he'd look into the matter and buy a little something at the fetish seller's stall: a protection against caimans, hippopotamuses, treacherous currents, and all the dangers presented by water. It worked for the Djoliba (a.k.a. Niger), Senegal, and Congo Rivers, but it hadn't ever been tested on the Atlantic. Since Sese didn't know how to swim, he really needed it—unless he found time to learn in the meantime. To brave a monster like the sea in a pirogue, it was better to protect yourself in advance. In three days—thanks to the efficient network within CEDEAO, the Community of West African States—he had left Lomé by road for Abidjan, courtesy of the STIF bus company. He spent a week in Abidjan, taking the opportunity to visit an uncle who had worked for Mobutu's DSF special presidential division. From there he took a TCV bus for Yamoussoukro, passed through Bobo-Dioulasso in Burkina Faso, then headed toward Bamako in Mali. With GANA

Transport he traveled to the Senegalese border and Kayes, finally arriving in Dakar, where he planned to secure a place on a pirogue for Almería, if he could pluck up the necessary courage.

~

Leaving Dramé's, Sese and Ichrak rejoined the uninterrupted bustle of Rue Goulmima: car horns sounding, hawkers calling out to customers, the crowds on the sidewalks going about their business. The two of them turned left, climbing back up the street opposite the arcades. The troublemakers stopped their games and watched them. The one in the Gucci cap brought his finger across his throat as he eyed Ichrak. She saw it.

"Are you threatening me?"

Before Sese realized what was going on and could stop her, she made a beeline for the other side of the street, paying no attention to the traffic. The drivers honked, barely avoiding a pileup. Curses flew from the vehicles. Beneath the arcades, the guys gestured to her to come closer, promising she'd see what she would see. That just made her twice as mad. Gawkers appeared. An altercation would relieve the tedium of the day. Ichrak stopped in the street a few yards from the men and set about hurling insults at them, forcing the cars to swerve around her. Sese tried to pull her away to the other sidewalk, so they could continue on their way, but Ichrak was out of control. Sese sensed a scene in the making, and in the present situation, especially at her side, he didn't think it was smart to linger. More and more people were gathering.

"Respect yourself, daughter. A woman shouldn't expose herself like that." This rebuke came from an old battle-ax in a fleece-lined tiger-stripe gandoura, shopping bag in hand.

"What do you expect? She gives herself to Africans," an old man put in. "She's no longer a woman!" He emphasized his point with a nod of his goatee.

"Keep shouting and you're dead meat, you crazy bitch!" said one of the hoodlums.

Ichrak was like a madwoman. Sese was unable to calm her. On the third floor of the building opposite, Dramé was signaling, begging the young woman to calm herself. The man with the expressive fingers pointed to the third floor and repeated his gesture.

"You won't do a thing to me! You think I'm afraid of you, you louse?" Ichrak yelled.

"She's not afraid of anything because she's a witch. Her mother too. Everyone in the neighborhood knows them," said the old man, who looked like a fake hajj.

"It's true!" the onlookers confirmed.

"Like mother, like daughter," the woman added, turning to the crowd for affirmation.

A little of everything was there: in the forefront were a large number of unemployed, because they obviously had nothing better to do and the show, with its guaranteed suspense, didn't cost a thing. Then there were children, and women doing their shopping. People elbowed for a better view. One group spilled over onto the roadway, where they caused a minor traffic jam. The car horns almost drowned the imprecations coming from the mouth of the young woman, whose hair was now disheveled; in her Adidas top, she looked like a boxer getting psyched up for a fight. She was hopping up and down, defying the thugs, who were hesitating, wondering how they could go for her, in the middle of this throng of pedestrians and automobiles.

"Get in!"

A car door opened. Without thinking, Sese bundled Ichrak into the vehicle, a white high-clearance Peugeot 5008 SUV. He opened the rear door and tumbled inside, slamming the door behind him at once. The driver set off.

"You saw how they were talking to me?"

The young woman was still raging.

"You shouldn't get upset like that, Ichrak. We almost got killed!" said Sese. "In any case, thank you, monsieur. Without you, I don't know how . . . It was close."

Cherkaoui was frowning at Ichrak, as if assessing the damage. She looked fine.

"They're not worth it, Ichrak. Cool down. I happened to be passing through the neighborhood; I wasn't expecting to see you. You need to be careful with crowds, they're capable of anything."

"Screw them! Thank you, Si Ahmed."

She'd found her smile again. She was really lucky to have him by her side.

"Where are you headed, Sese? Do you want to be dropped off at your place?"

"Yeah, I'm kind of in shock. I think I need to rest up a bit. I'll go back home—to the 'palace in Palestine' as they say."

The car screeched out of Rue Goulmima, reached Place d'Alexandrie, and descended toward the sea along Boulevard Mohamed Zerktouni, so everyone could take a breath on Boulevard Sidi Mohamed Ben Abdellah. To the left, the ocean extended, wave upon wave. The air streamed in through the open windows, blowing on the young people's faces and calming them—they felt like they were out at sea, being swept along by the wind alone. Sese got out at the roundabout in front of the Hassan II mosque. He took the opportunity to stroll for a while along the esplanade among the families and tourists looking for a bit of peace and quiet. He watched the waves of the Atlantic breaking against the rocks at the foot of the building, whose minaret rose almost seven hundred feet into the air. From a digital loudspeaker, the voice of the muezzin resonated all around, reassuring hearts, seeking to put things back where they belonged, at their right time.

It had been an intense day for Ichrak, but for the first time someone had come to her rescue at the exact moment needed. Her brain had caught fire just before, and now she could feel the flames dying and slowly becoming embers. These, though, took longer to go out. That was how she was. In the room on Rue Cénacles des Solitudes, she lay down on her stomach and put her head on her crossed arms. Ahmed Cherkaoui was sitting on the edge of the bed, gently stroking her hair. The place was quiet; the sound of the few cars that passed barely reached them. Cherkaoui said nothing, waiting for her to fully be herself again. He'd been present at the incident but didn't know what it was about. He'd brought her back to his studio apartment, sensing that she needed a refuge for a few minutes or a few hours. She shifted and turned on her side. Cherkaoui got up and sat in the armchair at the foot of the bed.

"Are you feeling better? Who were those people?"

"Asses! They think they can lay down the law wherever they want, with anybody. Not with me!"

"You're hurting yourself, Ichrak. You have to be careful with guys like that. Even if you're in the right, with riffraff of that kind, there's no reasoning. You have to understand that, *habibi*."

Ichrak threw Cherkaoui a keen look with a slight smile in the corner of her eye. She rested her head on the pillow, wriggled a little to find the most comfortable position, and closed her eyes.

"Do you want to sleep for a bit? Don't mind me."

She didn't respond.

Ichrak didn't want to sleep. She wanted to dream. Of a father, for instance. She was entitled to, since she'd never had one of her own. You never get used to it—to living without one. Ichrak knew the pain it caused. When she was little, she often thought she'd spotted him on the street, though she knew nothing about him. She'd never heard the least mention of him, the least name whispered in another room. As concerned

Zahira, it was impossible to make her say anything. "It's none of your business!"—such was her perpetual reply. As if he'd never existed. Yet he must be somewhere. If he were dead, someone would have said something, thought Ichrak. This fact had become a fantasy as immaterial as smoke, and like smoke it gradually filled her being. Having no description of him, from time to time she imagined seeing him—in someone of the right age who would pay attention to her in a disinterested way, somebody she'd never seen before but who was asking questions about her mother, or simply some charismatic person who was obviously worthy of being the progenitor she was awaiting like a messiah: you believe firmly in him but you're sure you'll never see his coming. Yet she deserved to have him, she thought. And what father would not be proud to have her as his daughter?

And here Cherkaoui had entered her life without warning. He took an interest in her, asked the occasional question about her mother, and he had authority and elegance. In addition, since they'd known one another, he'd never uttered a word out of place or made any sort of vulgar move. Ichrak had put him to the test once or twice, and he'd stayed true to himself. He wasn't after her body—of that Ichrak was sure by now. She didn't really understand what he did want from her, but what she knew was that he needed to see her as much as she needed to see him. Ichrak kept her eyes closed to be able to pursue her dream, in which she was no longer abandoned. She listened to Cherkaoui, though he made no sound, sitting in the armchair at her feet. After a moment he got up, took a few steps, trying to be quiet, reached into the young woman's handbag, and took out her MP3 player. He went back to the armchair, put the headphones on, and pressed the play button. He leaned back, closed his eyes in turn, and listened to the recording of *At the Origin Our Obscure Father*, by the novelist Kaoutar Harchi.

Ichrak hadn't moved, but she heard the click of the player. In her head, she began to recite:

I think the dawn is here. Its blinding light. And there's the reflection. At the far end of the room, in the full-length mirror, we're both reflected. I mumble something, pale beneath my makeup and my mascara, which has run. Now you need to rest, I whisper in my father's ear. I'll come back and see you again soon. The Father stretched out on the bed, slowly. I put a cushion under his head. I took a clean sheet and blankets from the closet, covered him solicitously and, as he requested, I passed him his rosary of white pearls. I stroked his cheek and, without a sound, I moved toward the door, took hold of the handle, pulled it open, then I left. But from where? From that room? From a dream?

~

If emotions had come to a climax, it was because in the meantime, under attack from the currents of Africa, the Gulf Stream had had to beat a retreat toward the North Atlantic, forcing Climate Change to scatter. Because of this, the Canary Current and the nor'easterly trades erected a sort of rampart around the Tropic of Cancer, to the east of the Azores High—the zone controlled by Chergui. These two influences created a larger tropospheric space within which Chergui was able to move forward, activating huge areas of low pressure that could be seen in the way the palm trees lining the avenues danced to its glory, tousled by gusts of wind, like an illustration of its power and at the same time of human frailty when a dreamlike breath plays its part in inflaming human feelings.

6

LOW PRESSURE

UNDER THE ARCADES ON RUE GOULMIMA, the cafés were packed. In one of them, the customers, drinking tea or coffee, were arguing loudly over games of cards or dominoes. The waiters, tray balanced on one hand above their head, dodged among those entering or leaving or others standing by and commenting on the games. Strangely, you would have sworn that all of them were taking care not to get too close to a table where Nordine Guerrouj sat with Yacine Barzak. A sort of no-man's-land had formed spontaneously around them. The two men were known in the neighborhood, and no one had any wish to overhear what they might be saying to one another. Even breathing the same air was to be avoided, since it could be held against you now or in the future. If these men were known to be dangerous, the people responsible for their present meeting were a great deal more so. Guerrouj and Barzak were vicious, everyone knew, but not as much as the wolves that were seeking to expand their hunting grounds—the latter exerted a heavy pressure that could be felt in the ecosystem.

"Have you tried using religion?"

"All I know about that is 'Allahu Akbar' and 'bismillah,' Nordine. To kick them out using religion, go around saying Africans are infidels—you'd need to be an imam at the least, I'm telling you. It's impossible to scare them enough. They're glued to their homes. It's not going to be easy to make them leave."

"Then all you have to do is tell people they're thieves."

"I'm the king of thieves myself; who's going to listen to me? You're stressing too much, Nordine. Be patient; we just need to wait for the right opportunity, dammit. Then we can do all the stirring you like. I'll burn down the buildings with the Africans still inside, if need be, and that'll be the last you'll hear of them. But while we're waiting, let God do his thing; he's the one making the decisions." Yacine pointed toward the ceiling since he didn't know which direction Mecca was in.

Farida had given Nordine an ultimatum. He wasn't mistaken; he knew those kinds of women. Since she never let anything show, you could never tell how far her resentment really went, nor her influence for that matter. Even if Mme Azzouz set Guerrouj's flesh on fire, his instinct told him to be afraid of her. As for Yacine Barzak, he'd long been forced to jettison such superfluous things as emotions. Forty years old, with a weaselly face topped with a little knockoff Gucci cap and a matching bag slung across his shoulder, he wore jeans and a PSG soccer shirt. It was a boyish outfit, but that was only to mislead people into thinking he was harmless—something quite impossible, since he'd grown up on the streets of Casablanca among other children of his kind and since his teenage years had gotten his education at the Oukacha prison, where, precisely, all emotions were inevitably pared away. There, if you saw something or heard something, you acted as if nothing had happened. You had to deny any feeling inside yourself. At first you did it so as not to get out of your depth, then later simply to survive.

The café was buzzing with conversation. No one could make out the words of the two crooks busy plotting away, but nothing good was likely to come from their meeting. All the more so because, despite long rap sheets and profiles littered with vile deeds, God—buried under vast numbers of such dossiers, scouring them for some act of mercy—is unable, like most of us, to attend to everything at once, and in such a way he lets a great many villains flourish at their ease.

～

Ahmed Cherkaoui perched on the edge of the bed, face in hands, shoulders shaking. He'd been sitting there helplessly for twenty minutes, in the quiet of the bedroom, struggling to contain the emotion that was sweeping over him. He had been completely unaware. For several days he'd been trying to get in touch with Ichrak without success. She hadn't answered her phone and hadn't called him back. It was rare that he went without hearing from her for so long. Since he couldn't approach her mother directly, he'd decided to go make inquiries in Derb Taliane. There he learned what had happened. A dark void opened up before him, as if a path had come to an end and it wasn't possible to turn back. He tried to get a grip on himself. He heard Farida's car on the gravel outside the villa. He went into the bathroom, and standing in front of the mirror, he saw that the tragedy had suddenly aged him. He splashed cold water on his face over and over, trying to clear his head. When he felt he could confront the world again, he dried himself and headed toward the day room, guided by the smell of Farida's heady perfume.

In recent months she'd dressed exclusively either in black or in white. This evening, she was wearing an immaculate Victoria Beckham outfit with white patent leather Louboutins. She hadn't yet put down her Céline handbag. She was talking, standing in the middle of the room, her back to Cherkaoui.

Always that phone, he thought to himself.

"*Shukran*—thank you, my friend! *Slama!*" she concluded, her voice velvety smooth.

She turned to her husband.

"Good grief, what's the matter?" she exclaimed. "You look like you've seen a ghost."

Cherkaoui was a little disconcerted. He tried to ignore the question.

"Tell me, Cherka," she pressed him.

"Young Ichrak is dead."

"I see! And that's why you're in such a state? I heard about it. It's been two or three weeks, no?"

"You knew and you didn't say anything?"

"I had no idea she was so important to you. And I thought you had heard. Actually, I was going to talk to you about it."

"You were going to talk to me about it? You knew I cared about her. How many times have you made a scene over her."

"Well, now at least you'll be spared that."

"Don't be mean, Farida. You have no idea what there could have been between that girl and me. In fact, you'd never understand. Just like I have no idea what there could be between you and those men you're always meeting."

"I'm just taking care of business, habibi. What could they mean to me? But you—what business did you have with the daughter of Al Majnouna?"

"Don't force me to go into details, or to talk about the marks I saw on your skin that I did not make. So you know Zahira, on top of everything? It wouldn't surprise me if you'd been to see her. You want everything."

"You're mistaken. Though lots of people consult her. You think I should do the same? I feel that you've been distant, these last days. You think she could do something for us?"

Cherkaoui stared at her for a few seconds, then, in exasperation, headed toward the front door, saying, "Don't wait for me; I'll eat out."

He left his home neighborhood of Anfa, took Avenue Assa, and turned into Ain Diab and the coast road. Traffic was usually smooth outside of rush hour. Cherkaoui was driving at random.

He'd said he wanted to go get dinner, but he didn't have anywhere special in mind, and in any case a restaurant was not what he was after. He wanted above all just to be out of the house. As well as easing his pain, he felt a need to find out more on the subject of Ichrak. He'd put so much into their relationship, and he missed her terribly at the moment. His grief was profound, and he hadn't come to terms with it. The loss of someone close to us is always hard, Cherkaoui had known that for a long time, but something more linked him to the young woman: her mother, Zahira. Neither Ichrak nor Farida knew it, but he had loved her once, long ago. At a certain moment, she'd refused to see him anymore, then had abruptly disappeared. He never knew why. She had always refused to believe that he'd ever get more involved with her. She had probably been right. Later, he learned that she'd had a child, a little girl, and he'd wished her all possible happiness. But ten years later, he'd seen Zahira again. She was a mere shadow of her former self. It was as if she'd lived too long or had had one experience too many. People already regarded her as a madwoman. He had turned the other way.

His phone rang. He reached into his jacket pocket.

"Yes?"

"What did you mean by 'marks you saw on my skin'?"

"Listen, Farida—"

"What did you see? And what do you mean by that? Are you implying that someone left finger marks on my skin? Do you take me for a whore, Cherka?"

"That's what you're calling me about? To ask me that?"

"Say it if that's what you think, Ahmed. If you paid a little more attention to that skin . . . Don't you get it? I gave you my life, Ahmed!"

"Cut it out; this isn't the time. I'm driving." The sound of car horns around him called him to attention. "I can't talk now; I'll call you later."

He hung up.

Farida was furious. She sent the phone spinning across the room. It smashed against the wall, but still not satisfied, she tossed a pillow at the shattered pieces lying on the ground. After expressing herself in this way, she snatched up the wine glass that stood on the bedside table, where there was also a tray with an almost untouched meal, drained the glass in one gulp and poured herself another at once.

"'You knew I cared about her.' You don't care about *me* anymore!" she raged.

She sat back where she'd been, propped at the head of the bed, her back against a heap of pillows.

"On top of which, he has the gall to talk to me about those men, whereas what does he usually say? He acts like he doesn't give a damn. Bastard! I hate you, Ahmed!" she yelled.

To compose herself, she picked up the remote and turned on the TV that faced the bed. That would distract her. She chanced on a Turkish serial with a story line interweaving business, love, and betrayal. Farida followed the plot, but very quickly her thoughts strayed. She had trouble loosening up. She hated any kind of vexation. An only child, she had always been spoiled in almost every way. With beauty, intelligence, and money to begin with, the rest was supposed to follow without too much effort. That was how Cherkaoui had come into her life. At the time, he was an actor. All the women fought over him, so naturally Farida had thought that she alone should be the one he came home to. Meeting him once at a reception had been enough. He'd succumbed immediately to her spell. From that moment, she'd been absolutely certain he would be hers; he was good-looking, there was something tough in his expression, he was open, he knew how to talk to her, and with time, she even enjoyed considerable freedom. He'd had no plans to settle down, but she was an enterprising woman, and the marriage was celebrated with great pomp.

The ground was laid for a true fairy tale, except that the fairy who watched over Farida thought rather about jewelry, gowns, cars, and villas and neglected the matter of offspring. After years of trying unsuccessfully, the couple were forced to accept the facts: Farida could not conceive. She threw herself into work and parties, but questions began to emerge. She wondered if Ahmed wouldn't drop her in the end and marry a younger woman who'd guarantee him an heir. With that anxiety, Farida's self-confidence was shaken. She began to question her husband's love for her and even to doubt her own beauty, though most of the men in Casa jostled at her feet to pay zealous tribute. She liked that. She even learned to turn it to a very agreeable profit while waiting to win back Ahmed's love as she had enjoyed it before.

Cherkaoui had decided to simply drive; for the moment the road would determine his route.

Why did I have to go and get attached to that girl? he asked himself in anger.

He too had been somewhat spoiled by life. As a young actor he'd been a huge success on national television and in a handful of movies. That was when he'd met Zahira. It was true that she would have found it hard to fit in with his circle. She wasn't part of any circle herself; she was unique and endowed with a fiery temperament. Ahmed had no control over the situation and for that reason was a little afraid. Nor could he say, even in his wildest romantic fantasies, that she might have been the woman of his life, because he'd known many others subsequently. In the meantime, he married Farida. Later, he took charge of the Espace des Amdiaz theater company and began to direct. His work, helped by occasional interventions on the part of Farida's father and his friends—public funding was essential in developing creative work—included the mounting of particular productions. In this way he was able to maintain the standing of his theater and his directorial reputation for putting on the most innovative plays and performances. He had to admit that when, with time, existential thoughts on both sides had induced a crisis in his marriage, his successful career came to his aid in furnishing an excuse to get away from time to time and to set his heart on younger actresses looking for new perspectives on their work. But he had tired of that too. All he wanted was peace and quiet, and his moments with Ichrak provided exactly that. In front of him, in the middle of the broad boulevard, half a dozen young men revving large-engined bikes were racing up and down, speeding up to one hundred miles per hour for short stretches, then braking abruptly. Other drivers made room for them: today's fantasia had to take place. Helmetless in the moonlight, with an infinite confidence in life, they did wheelies, the frame of the machine rising upward like crazy, handlebars and front wheel whizzing flashily in the air. They zoomed by smartly on their back wheel alone, like a challenge to death and to the universal laws of gravity.

The affection Cherkaoui felt for Ichrak had nothing to do with Zahira. It was simply his time of life. Now that oaths had become obsolete and dreams unreachable, he found himself turning toward obsession, his heart inclining toward essential things or sometimes love, that merciless feeling that does not belong to you and that, one day, alights on someone you haven't even actually chosen.

"Can I help you?"

"Thank you, but I'm just looking."

Cherkaoui could never forget the moment he met Ichrak for the first time. It was the final day of the reading of Kaoutar Harchi's book *At the Origin Our Obscure Father*. The young woman was staring at a photo of the author among press reviews and posters for the show. She'd found herself there by chance: she'd been walking near Place Zellaqa, had taken some random street to get to Boulevard Mohammed V with its row of art deco buildings, and had ended up in front of the display window of a theater.

"She's really beautiful, and her expression is extraordinary."

"The author? Yes. And she's incredibly gifted. She must be about your age, yet she has an extraordinary sensitivity when it comes to the intimate feelings of men and women."

What had drawn Cherkaoui to Ichrak was the sometimes extravagant life force that emanates from a person in the process of becoming. From the moment he set eyes on her, he had sensed it keenly—specifically in the intensity of her gaze.

"Do you fancy seeing the show this evening? It's the last performance. I can leave your name at the box office if you like."

"I can't make it this evening; I have to stay home. My mother isn't well. But my name is Ichrak."

"'Rising sun.' It suits you. Ichrak what, if I might ask?"

"I don't have any other name."

"Ichrak is right for you. It's the moment when the angels of the day take over from those of the night. It's a powerful name. Like the star that rises on the horizon."

"It's the name my mother chose for me. I have to go now."

And that had been all. On that day, what Cherkaoui had experienced was indeed something like a sunrise. But he hadn't yet understood its full import; things are written of their own accord while we ourselves still have our doubts.

They had met up again a few times. He picked up a little more about her, here and there—above all about the mystery that was her birth, since she was the fatherless daughter of Zahira. Later on, one time they met on the terrace of a café; as a souvenir of their first encounter, Cherkaoui had brought a little MP3 player with a recording of the reading of *At the Origin Our Obscure Father*. He gave it to her, and stars lit up in Ichrak's eyes, her smile adding yet another touch of brilliance. After they told one another about their respective lives, especially Ichrak's, he got around to asking her age. She was twenty-eight. Cherkaoui's heart leapt in his chest and from that moment never calmed when he thought of her.

Zahira had disappeared; then she had had her baby. Ichrak was born in June, she told him. Cherkaoui's brain made a rapid calculation of its own accord: she'd come into the world nine months after his last evening with Zahira. They hadn't made love that night but had done so three days before and the following day too. It was etched in his memory—he'd been rehearsing for the opening of the new theater season. Even without admitting it to himself, from that moment Ahmed Cherkaoui was secretly convinced that Ichrak was the fruit of his own flesh. The idea imposed itself in a visceral, irrational manner. He looked for points of resemblance. Eventually he found one that went to the core: it was their shared love of text and Ichrak's capacity for being inhabited by words, just like him. He even imagined her on stage, performing in her solemn voice. Back then, though, he hadn't noticed anything particularly significant, but for a brief instant he'd thought he recognized a fleeting gesture. After he paid, they got up. As he left her, Cherkaoui hoped that the sublime words of Kaoutar Harchi might help to put a little meaning in what he knew of the harsh path of Ichrak's life.

⁓

Everyone did in fact know Al Majnouna, and Farida was no exception. A few months earlier, in a moment of doubt, late one evening she'd gone to consult her. When Zahira opened the door, her gaze did not linger on her visitor. She turned her back on her at once. Yet she'd immediately recognized Farida Azzouz, wife of Ahmed Cherkaoui. Always dressed with extreme elegance, she was wearing a silk headscarf and, as often, was clad in black. In the middle of the small living room, she had taken off the scarf, releasing a cloud of perfume. For Zahira it was the smell of money. She turned around.

Her clientele was diminishing with time, and rich women no longer came regularly to see her. When they visited, it was invariably about soured love affairs in which it was imperative to win back the heart, and above all the senses, of the swine who had grown distant. These were not Zahira's favorite clients. She knew that such cases were difficult: usually, the guy was stuck between the thighs of a rival, and when that was so, it was virtually impossible to regain the advantage, except when they paid through the nose to hear words of hope. Aside from such desperate women, she was only ever consulted by the poor of the neighborhood for whom praying had ceased to be effective. For many of them, becoming rich was largely out of the question, but they could at least employ spells to try to remove whichever person lay in the path of acquiring wealth. Since God was merciful, prayers didn't work in this regard, and Al Majnouna would intervene; putting a hex on someone was one of her specialties. In that, poor and rich were alike: anything could happen to a rival grappling with a curse. This sort of job paid rather well, and Zahira could take her time without worrying that her client would walk out on her in dissatisfaction, because—as everyone knows—nothing is as tenacious as hatred.

Fate was sometimes mischievous. Zahira would never have thought that one day she'd open her door to Cherkaoui's wife. The woman had everything: wealth, a husband who loved her—a serious and dependable man. Why would she come to see Zahira?

"Sit down," she said, indicating the window seats.

Farida sat.

"Let me make you some tea."

She moved off toward the pots and pans lying on a dresser in the alcove. Farida looked around the room. The walls were decorated with friezes in blue. Apart from that, there were only day beds, cushions, a leather pouf. There were no electrical appliances, no radio, not even a clock on the wall. Farida shouldn't have come, but the situation at home was out of control. Ahmed was getting away from her. He came home late more often than before, and on such evenings he seemed absent—Farida had trouble getting his attention. She'd also occasionally smelled perfume on him. Not an expensive perfume that could have lingered after he greeted someone from his milieu but a cheap knockoff of the kind bought by working people. Farida had her suspicions that her husband had had affairs during their marriage. In his younger days he'd been a ladies' man, and he still had his charms—even more so since he'd settled down, and his self-possession made him even more attractive. The perfume worried her. It was likely worn by a young woman, probably rather pliant, with the fieriness of her youth. All this left her with little that was concrete. Farida wanted to shed some light on the situation, and Zahira could, if not actually identify a possible rival and counteract her, then at least revive her husband's desire for his wife. At her age, it was best to stack the deck as much as possible in her own favor.

"It's been cold these last nights. My rheumatism's been playing up—you have no idea."

Zahira limped around, the way she always did during a visit. It was a matter of throwing them off, especially with Cherkaoui's wife. Her clients needed her, but the last thing she wanted was for them to think she was doing well out of it. In the popular subconscious, there was a strong conviction that in order to attain certain knowledge and to practice the specialties that Zahira did, it was absolutely essential to sacrifice your soul, or at least a good portion of it, to one of the numerous demons that fought over the spoils in hell. Concluding such a pact could never bring you well-being in the visible world, and Zahira felt that this should be plain to see. The money her patients offered her served mostly to ease their conscience, making the transaction feel like an exchange of favors that at bottom was insignificant in the eyes of God and society rather than an actual foray into the world of evil.

"We're never safe. You're a woman who's been spoiled by life; that much is plain. But you're generous; I feel that you do everything to make those around you happy. Some of them don't repay you the way they should. You're very beautiful, but you're missing something. Your heart is suffering. You adore love. And you want more of it. The water is on for the tea, my daughter; we have plenty of time. Tell me: Is it your husband?"

Her hands held in Zahira's, who was sitting facing her on the pouf, Farida Azzouz opened up, speaking of her worries, of the way she and her husband had drifted apart, something she could not understand. She wanted to know for sure whether he had someone else; she sensed it, but she'd come here to seek certainty. Zahira nodded in assent and in sympathy. She spoke of the fickleness of men, who can crumble the moment some slender woman walks by.

"They're capable of anything when it happens to them. You see some of them go to ruin; others hang themselves," she added, miming holding a rope above her head. "But you have to watch out; they can just as well kill you. Some of them have the evil in them," she warned, narrowing her eyes.

She stopped herself quickly, because it was important to maintain hope in her client. Now they had reached a ground of understanding; the conversation warmed up noticeably.

"He neglects me," Farida admitted.

"I sensed it the moment you came in. I can help you; that's not hard. But there's something else. Let me first consult those who manage our lives. The other thing is money, isn't it?"

"My business affairs," Farida specified. "Things keep changing. I have to be on my toes. The men I deal with are so tough."

"So are you."

"But I don't want them to see it."

"You're not just beautiful; you're smart too. I can arrange for you to be invisible when you wish it. Those men are nothing; you hold all the aces. You can be even more irresistible. But there are things you mustn't do, taboos you need to respect. No more coffee, no more wine. You'll stop seeing your friends. Don't lend anyone anything, and going to bed is out of the question."

Farida said nothing.

"Do you understand me? Do you understand what this means?"

"Of course."

At this moment, Zahira began to speak in a language that resembled Arabic but was not. Farida listened, trying to make out if it was a dialect, but this was something different. It sounded like a prayer, yet certainly neither God nor the angels spoke this tongue. Zahira got up, walked over to a low cabinet, and took from it a chased copper tray containing various objects: dried vegetables, a few mummified organic remains, a clay ointment jar, small rocks of incense. She took one of these and lit it, put it back on the tray, made the smoke rise abundantly, then continued her soliloquy with the shadows. Still talking, she came back to Farida, sat down, and placed the tray on the floor. She picked up the little jar, opened it, put her fingers inside, and said, "Close your eyes and your mouth."

Farida complied. Zahira anointed her eyes, mouth, and forehead with an oily substance that smelled faintly of citronella.

"This also protects you from snakes and scorpions!" she said.

Her voice rose louder, but as if in a dialogue: she formed long sentences, then provided the answers herself in a whisper. The sounds coming from Al Majnouna's throat had grown hollow, as if someone else were speaking for her. During this time, she behaved as if Farida were no longer there. The latter was glad to have her eyes closed. In such a situation, the less you see the better. After this guttural exchange, Zahira seemed to calm down, but then she began murmuring in a sort of fearful voice; she must have been agreeing to mystical procedures. She took a little of the feces of a corpse, which she'd bought from the attendants at the morgue and had prepared and dried. She crumbled it between her thumb and forefinger, above the little block of incense. There was a dull pop, and through her closed eyelids, Farida noticed a flash.

"Open your eyes!"

When she did, Farida saw smoke rising above the tray and caught a strong smell of excrement. She grimaced in disgust. Zahira took some more of the oily substance on her finger and rubbed it vigorously under her client's nose. Farida recoiled, but her face relaxed immediately, and a smile appeared on her lips.

"I can't smell anything at all, not even the scent of lemon."

"That's what will happen to men who come near you: they'll no longer sense anything; they won't see or hear much at all, except you, your power, and the power of what I'll give you. Put it on your skin before you perfume yourself. Don't ever forget the perfume itself—that's what will conceal the charm and carry it all the way into their heart."

"It's Pure Poison, by Dior."

"It has power; it will accomplish its task. With my product and the perfume, you'll be irresistible in all things. Above all, don't change anything: those who are around us know it now. The men you'll have dealings with will hear words that seem to come from heaven. Your beauty and your feminine aura will be their trap. All you'll have to do is to be yourself."

Farida liked what she was hearing. Now she could take things as far as she herself wanted.

"As for your husband . . ." Farida's ears pricked up again. "In his case we don't even need to talk about it. You'll see for yourself this evening."

The night was quiet. A gusty wind was sweeping across the rooftops as a first sign from Chergui, which was soon to arrive. All that could be heard was the distant sound of traffic. Sitting on the terrace, Ichrak could hear the voices of her mother and the visitor. She'd caught the name of Cherkaoui, and overhearing a few details, she figured out that it was about the man she knew. So this was his wife. He always spoke of her respectfully. If she'd brought up his name with Ichrak's mother, it was because she didn't think she was happy in her marriage or that she wanted to tame him, as certain women like to do. She only hoped that Farida was not there on her account, Ichrak's. The voices had dropped; now the two women were whispering. Ichrak put her headphones back on and tried to go back to the story at a moment of heartache and rebellion.

I swung back and forth, on one foot. How can I not feel, each time she speaks of him, the twist in my heart, the faltering of my whole body? How can I not want her to continue the story of her life and clarify for me the mysteries that veil my own? Because about the recent furtive visit of the Father, the Mother has said nothing, no word of explanation. Of consolation. It's as if the Mother has forgotten. And has wished that I too should forget the very existence of that Father. You'd think the Mother made me all on her own.

7

HEAT WAVE

NEARLY THIRTY YEARS EARLIER, the neighborhood around the medina displayed its riches in alleyways where, more than today, feelings could be triggered at any turn. That's what had happened to Ahmed Cherkaoui when he encountered Zahira. At the time, she was twenty-four; he was thirty. He knew her, like everyone in the neighborhood did. A crazy woman it was best to avoid. She was partial to scandal, people said, but her insolent beauty drew everyone's attention. He'd already noticed her, though only from a distance. He'd grown up amid Casablanca's middle class, and the two of them moved in separate circles. This time, the narrowness of the street had forced them to brush past one another, to the point that Ahmed had smelled the emanations of the beautiful Zahira's body. In talking to her, he'd adopted the appropriate tone, the kind you use with an animal that hasn't yet been tamed, a tone in which you convey self-assurance but sound as conciliatory as possible. She had accepted the lemonade and the shade he'd proposed on a café terrace. From there, a fiery love story had evolved—the kind of fire that could only break out behind closed doors, when the lovers were alone.

"You'll never marry me. In this room you show me your passion, you speak of love, but are you prepared to display it to the world? By marrying me, for example? You won't accept the consequences, Ahmed. 'I love you, I love you'—that's all you can say."

"If I married you, you'd become like all the others; you'd no longer give me your body the way you do now. You're a delight, Zahira."

"You bastard, that's all you think about!"

She got out of bed, picked up the clothes that Ahmed had calmly removed a few minutes earlier, dressed, and left the room before he could make a valid case for himself.

That evening, Zahira went back into town and sauntered for a long while through the streets as far as Place Bab Marrakech. Aside from the distant echo of footsteps, the alleyways were plunged in silence. At a certain moment, her attention was drawn by snippets of music drifting by. She felt as if she was under a spell: the melody spoke to her soul. It was the beginning of the song "Seret El Hob"—Story of Love—by the great contralto Umm Kulthum. She followed the singing as she would have followed a star shining brighter than the rest.

La ana addi esh-shuq
Wi layali esh-shuq
Wa la albi addi azabu, azabu
Tol omri ba'ul.
I cannot bear longing
And nights of longing
And my heart can no longer take its torments
All my life, I say.

The voice was rough, and the singer broke off at the end of the verse. Exclamations followed.

"Be quiet! Don't overdo it. Stick to drinking."

"You're right."

The man helped himself to a glass of wine and downed it in one.

"I need to loosen my vocal cords," he said in self-justification.

He cleared his throat and resumed the song about the feeling of love, which can overwhelm you. After the first bar, the others egged him on with cries and joined in with their instruments.

At the corner of the street, Zahira had recognized the diva's song, and the performance had touched her. The tune was being interpreted with an almost violent spontaneity very different from the controlled voice of the original recording. She pushed on a half-open door that led to a small courtyard. Four men had gathered there, each holding a musical instrument. The oud player sent the young woman a welcoming smile. He was handsome and a little sinister, though a moustache softened his expression. The tabla drummer wore a police uniform—the courtyard was situated behind a government building, and these men must be city cops. He was playing at a furious rhythm, eyes closed, head bowed, so he could hear each beat, make sure it was precise. A fiddler with a scrawny face and a thin moustache stared at the young woman as his bow slid over the strings of his traditional *kwamanja*, while a *bendir* kept time to a syncopated beat. The instrumental music—the oud was fashioning a solo— filled Zahira's head for four more bars, then stopped abruptly at a sign from the oudist.

"Come closer, *ma belle*. Who are you? Don't be afraid. You're not lost; come, we're here. Plus, once the wine is drawn, it has to be drunk, you know," he added, pouring himself another glassful, his instrument resting in his lap.

The musician had seen the sparks dancing in the woman's eyes. Since they weren't enough on their own for a proper fire to start, they needed to be fed with some fuel.

"Have a drink! What's your name?"

Zahira hesitated as she reached for the glass, but she picked it up all the same and drank half of it in a single gulp. The oudist sensed that she was tense. The music must have lured her with a hope of comfort. The man reckoned that the wine and the music would not be enough to bring her the cure she sought. For pressure to be relieved, it has to be pushed to the breaking point. The man knew she was not far from that moment. Striking up the music again, he rose to his feet in a burst of laughter and placed his broad back against Zahira's back. The taps of the tabla had acted on the young woman's nervous system, urging her hips into movement, and her body seemed to be in the process of breaking up in fits and starts, in its center, in a controlled manner. She began a languorous dance, with all her bust, arms raised, hands fluttering like the wings of a butterfly in flight. At that moment the oudist was roaring with laughter, fingers gripping his instrument, chest raised skyward. The fiddler also got up, while the bendir player filled a glass and lifted it to the lips of the dancers, who had to down it in one as he stared insistently at them. The woman did not have the right to refuse. She drank. The oudist began to dance, while the tabla let loose, its echoes multiplying through the air. The dancer leaned back, pressing against the back and buttocks of the woman, until he no longer felt any resistance to the jerks he was making as he rolled his wide shoulders against her. The alcohol Zahira had consumed, along with the music, had made her head spin. She closed her eyes and let herself be enveloped in the frenzy of the instruments. The oudist turned around, and his arms encircled the young woman without touching her, the oud hanging from one hand. His mouth sought Zahira's, and his head moved like a cobra preparing to immobilize its prey. The tabla pounded like the beating of a frantic heart. The woman swayed and tried to elude the man. At that moment the bendirist rose too. He moved around the couple in a dance step, followed by the tabla player with the stern face, who stomped on the ground the way you grind spices with a pestle: heavy, hard, relentless.

The oudist was no longer smiling. His nostrils were quivering, and he looked as if he could pierce the young woman's skin with his gaze alone. His body held Zahira's close, and he forced her to the edge of the table on which he had just laid his instrument. Now the man's breath burned her neck. The strident sound of the fiddle curved in a tumultuous melody, feeling like claws inside the woman's belly. Her hips had not ceased moving. She was elsewhere. The bendirist had shifted to her right and was dancing, his arms extended. At that moment the sound of the tabla became harsher; Zahira's senses could no longer take in anything else but that and the breathing of the men surrounding her. The bendir player took her by the waist, as if in invitation. She was no longer dancing but was being tossed from one body to another. The oudist went on dancing, holding her hands in the air. The tabla player took this as a signal and tried to push the woman back against the table. Zahira resisted, fending off the arms that were trying to restrain her. She twisted away from them, and in her attempt to break loose, she knocked the oud off the table. It hit the ground with a terrible noise, followed by a chord like a tearing sound, caused by all the strings reverberating at the same time. The oudist's eyes flashed. He took a firm grip on the woman's wrists. The fall of the instrument had crystalized the anger that was beginning to form in him, and he let it show.

"All we wanted to do was play with you, and you go and break my oud? Just like that? Do you know what that means?"

Emotions were running high. Zahira's wide-eyed stare reflected the man's rage.

"Please," she begged. "Please let me leave."

The sound of her rising voice put a seal on things. The oudist slapped a large hand over her mouth, while his other hand took hold of her thigh and lifted it to the level of the tabletop. She fought back frenziedly. She tried to bite the hand that was smothering her, and a piercing cry came from her throat. In an effort to silence her, the oudist slapped her with a swinging blow. Its violence was such that Zahira's body instantly went limp, abandoning all resistance. That night, if the star she could have entrusted herself to, or followed, had put on its most shimmering gown, casting a thousand sparks into the firmament, it was not to guide Zahira's sensitive heart but only to be the brightest and most desirable at the ball of Betelgeuse, Aldebaran, and the Pleiades, which alas was taking place at that exact moment.

The slap had brought a sudden end to the murmurs and guffaws. One look was enough for the other musicians to know that from now on the matter would be settled exclusively between the woman and the oudist. The latter brusquely parted her thighs as he shouted, "Who told you to come here?"

He lowered his zipper, fumbled in his pants, took out his member, and, with a strong grip, set about searching for her opening. The tension he'd sensed earlier would serve him well; moistness would open the way for him—so he reasoned. His body lay upon hers, his eyes fixed upon a blue tattoo of a moon with crescents on either side, which her loosened clothing had revealed on the curve of her right shoulder, and in which he thought only of burying his teeth.

--

Slowly, I approach the kitchen door to see the shadow close up. I notice a hand. The thick hand of the shadow placing on the table a loosely tied-up piece of meat and like furies, the women push past me and burst into the kitchen. Forgetting the hand, forgetting the shadow, the women throw themselves fiercely on the slab of meat. Then the shadow vanishes, leaving me alone, devastated, a gaping hole in my chest.

When she listened to the text recorded on the MP3 player Cherkaoui had given her, Ichrak had understood that she wasn't the only one to live with the questions that obsessed her, affecting her heartbeat, leading her astray as they stole her thoughts away.

Without waiting any longer, I put my clothes back on and gathered my belongings one by one, hurried back to the room without a window, and turned the key twice to lock myself inside. I closed my eyes and implored the Father to come and get me.

With the passing years, the feeling did not lessen, and the lack was like a huge abyss that could not be filled.

Ichrak was sitting on her couch. Zahira sat on the one opposite. She was leaning on one elbow and seemed to be saying something to her daughter, pointing her finger at her. Ichrak took off the headphones and said, "What do you want now?"

"You're earning money, and you never give me anything—me, your own mother! I don't even have anything to wear; look at me. I barely eat; I have to go begging in the streets. Shame on you! It's no way to treat your old mother. I'm the one who brought you into the world." Zahira dug her fingers into her belly as if she wanted to tear out her innards. "You have no sense of gratitude; I had to raise you all on my own! Because of you, people called me names, humiliated me. They threw rocks at me, called me a witch, a prostitute. You never should have come into the world!"

"Stop it, you'll make me as crazy as you are!" screamed Ichrak.

"You dare to complain? I'm the one who should be complaining; I'm your lifeline. You don't give me a moment's peace, Mother. You brought me up alone because you wanted to. What did you do with my father? Where is he?"

"I don't owe you any explanations."

"You think not? You *do* owe me; you owe me half my life."

"You want to kill me, is that it? I sense it in what you give me to eat. The other day, the meal tasted funny."

The old woman retreated against the wall with the look of a frightened child. She whispered words that Ichrak couldn't make out, as usual. She turned to face the wall, still muttering. The young woman had had enough. She hurried up the narrow staircase that led to the rooftop terrace.

"Money, always money!" With her paltry income, Ichrak looked after her mother as best she could. She didn't skimp on anything. In fact, the medications soaked up almost all she earned. They were absolutely necessary because, even with them, the attacks of madness were unbearable. The doctors said that diabetes could have unexpected mental side effects, but Ichrak knew that it was her mother's life itself that had led to these excesses.

That life was a great mystery to the young woman. She knew little about it—only that Zahira had been born and raised in the neighborhood. Her beauty had been the cause of many problems. What had that man, Ichrak's begetter, been to her? Today, every movement of the young woman without a father was closely watched. When she walked out, she often overheard two or more people talking as they stared openly at her. Ichrak dreamed of an important man whose power would be feared to the point that no one would ever dare divulge his secret. Otherwise, how was such a mystery possible? Unless Zahira had had multiple lovers in her youth. As far back as she could remember, Ichrak's mother had always been mad. Even as a child, Ichrak had had to fend for herself. Zahira would go out and return with money for food, but Ichrak never knew how she got it. Did she go begging? Or do something else? She also received clients, but did that bring in enough for everything? And there was the house they lived in, which belonged to her and about which she said merely, "I was loved."

If the stars were shining that night in the firmament, Ichrak couldn't see them because the sky was obscured by the mass of sand brought from the desert. A burning-hot breeze swept over the rooftops, from which there was a view of terraces as far as the eye could see, as well as a multitude of satellite dishes like lunar discs in the night. Ichrak settled on a rug out of the wind. She pressed the play button and went back to listening to the girl's story from Kaoutar Harchi's *At the Origin Our Obscure Father*. The melody of the text unfurled in her head and, for a while, transported her toward a world where the shared pain of another could at least in some small fashion assuage her own suffering. In this way Ichrak's soul could rise a little, could fly up into the sky, despite the turmoil roiling her breast. The story flowed and branched within her.

Motionless on a stair, in the dark, for a long time I have the feeling that I'm still in the Father's bedroom, hearing his breathing, seeing each beat of his heart, smelling him on my clothes, his gaze fastened on the white lace-trimmed dress, re-living that experience of dying and then of coming back from among the dead. I was waiting for you, he murmurs.

෴

He had had to leave. Slimane Derwich had once again received a visit from the lovely Noor so that together they could analyze the work of Assia Djebar, and it had been an even greater disaster. Now she would certainly never come to his place again. Besides, his standing in her eyes was definitively wrecked. He hadn't known how to go about things. They'd been sitting, each in a chair, and Slimane had had to open the discussion, but it had been too much for him because the same scene as before had repeated itself, and this time Noor was wearing diaphanous fabrics colored cream and pearl that rendered her more lovely still, the gray glowing in the dimness of the room. She was just as reserved, her hands crossed demurely on the book in her lap. As they exchanged ideas about the role of literature in the struggle for independence, she had grown animated, and it was then that the catastrophe began: her copy of *Woman without Sepulcher* slipped off the silky material of her dress and fell to the floor. Slimane bent down to pick it up, she unhappily did the same, and that which should not have happened did happen: the contact between the young woman's fingers and Slimane's acted as a detonator, shattering his self-control. He forgot Noor, the embodiment of feminine grace; disregarding her oh so delicate movements, oblivious now to her extreme sensitivity, he took hold of her wrist in a vise-like grip.

"What are you doing?" she protested in a stifled cry.

Slimane, under pressure as he himself had diagnosed, seized the young woman bodily. With a twist of her chest, Noor broke free and stepped back, holding both hands in front of her as if for protection.

Derwich began, "Listen—"

"I don't think you'll see me here again, Monsieur Derwich! I only hope your behavior is not known at the university."

Her gaze permitted of no appeal. She turned on her heel, opened the door, and left without even closing it, leaving behind the work she had come to talk about. It was no longer "Monsieur Slimane," like a declaration of love, but "Monsieur Derwich." Slimane, who wanted to crawl into a hole and forget he even existed, needed all of his will to manage the two or three steps to the door. In the courtyard Noor was adjusting her headscarf and exchanging a few words with Mme Bouzid and Sese. At one point, all three turned in his direction. *Hashma*—shame— caused him to close the door at once, but not before he heard the young girl laugh at a remark by that upstart Congolese who never knew his place.

Till the evening, he stayed in his room like a convalescing patient, but at a certain moment he had to go out, feeling a need to be around other people. He went up Boulevard Sour Jdid, passed the naval school, took a right just before Rick's Café, and crossed the labyrinth of the old medina before coming out onto Rue Goulmima, drawn by the freshness of the air beneath the arcades. He sat down on his own at a café table. As he waited to be served, he thought about his grievances. Before him, the world continued to turn. On the roadway there were fewer and fewer cars, but those that were there enlivened the street with their lights and their horns. Streetsweepers were clearing the last of the refuse from the roadside. The stores were still lit, staying open into the night since there was a family to feed. A West African shayeur was passing among the tables, hawking pirate DVDs of the latest blockbusters. When he came to Slimane Derwich's table, the latter made a gesture as if chasing away a fly and said, "*Baad menni, azzi!* Get away from me, slave!"

The guy lingered; in all likelihood, he hadn't properly understood. But he was clearly pained—the tone alone had been enough to convey the speaker's intent. Slimane rose and shoved the man in the chest, forcing him away. The shayeur swore in Bambara and struck back. He sent Slimane spinning among the chairs; he landed flat on his back. The servers and other customers had to intervene. They pushed the other man out, as he shouted in French: "*Pourquoi?* Why?"

"They're dogs! What are we waiting for? They need to be dealt with once and for all."

Derwich turned to one of the men who'd helped him to his feet.

"Why should you have to buy that guy's trash and talk to him? The place isn't ours anymore. You were right to run him off; I'd have done the same."

The customer showing such concern wore a small Gucci cap and a PSG shirt. Yacine Barzak had swung by to check in on the apartment building opposite—he'd posted his men there in hopes of provoking the opportunity needed to get rid of the squatters. For several days, Guerrouj had firmly rejected the idea of setting fire to the buildings. The fact was that the insurance companies could hold things up for years, and that would be catastrophic. Terror was a better solution: then people would leave of their own accord. Harassment was no longer enough, and you always had to do the job yourself. He'd needed to come back in person for this excellent opportunity to arise, in the form of the person standing none too confidently in front of him. In any case, hearing the words of support, Slimane perked up: "They're vermin; they come here and take everything from us. Starting with our women!"

"You're telling me!" Pointing to the other side of the street, Barzak went on: "Over there, every day you see them coming and going, back and forth, from morning to night." He was making it up, building a picture of debauchery. "How much longer are we going to put up with it, us men? Is no one willing to get their hands dirty so the neighborhood can go back to being the way it used to be?"

"I am!" declared one of his sidekicks.

"Me too!" said another, as if acting out a script.

"You too, *khouya*, I feel it! You're someone important; you're educated—that's plain to see. We didn't like what just happened with that slave. I know where they are. Let's go!"

Barzak was holding Derwich by the elbow. Before the latter realized what was going on, a dozen or so individuals were crossing the street, pushing him along in front of them. They entered the apartment building opposite and went up to the third floor.

The northeast trades had not succeeded in joining up with those of the southeast that were supposed to move toward the North Atlantic. So Chergui, which originated in the far limits of the Sahara, had to pass via the equator and lodge an appeal with the one that controlled the most important axis in the South Atlantic: the mighty Benguela Current, born off the coast of the ancient kingdom of Kongo. It had to be asked to hold back the Canary Current and clear a passage to the east of the Azores High so Chergui could pursue its odyssey. The price that had to be paid for relieving the blockade on Casablanca, pushing past Gibraltar, and gaining access to the Mediterranean was that Benguela, in alliance with the Equatorial Current and the Brazil Current—the dominant forces to the north of the Roaring Forties and the Austral Current—crushed the offensive by the Gulf Stream and diverted Climate Change into a different theater of operations, provoking cyclones in Central America and the southern United States. This was made possible by the infiltrations of high-temperature currents originating in the southern hemisphere. The unleashing of two major hurricanes on the United States obliged the enemy to concentrate its forces on Texas and Florida, causing over $100 billion in damage and a loss of 1.5 percent of its GDP under the apocalyptic presidency of Donald Trump. But the battle for Ad-dar Al Baidaa' was still going on, and, with the temperature at over 110, exhaustion overcame the women's hearts, while fires burned in the men's.

In the narrow hallway on the third floor, a hammering on the door rose over the shouts and curses of the men armed with knives and clubs. At some point the jamb gave way, and the lock burst apart. The men charged into the room, blunt instruments swinging in the air. Dramé and the man who sometimes came with Abdoulaye tried to protect themselves or dodge out of the way, but there wasn't enough space. Fists rained down on heads, backs, ribs. The West Africans fell to the floor, utterly outnumbered.

"Tie them up!" Yacine shouted.

Their T-shirts were pulled off to serve as bonds. Lying on the ground like cattle, they twisted and turned, in vain.

"Hold them down!"

Hands seized the two men's limbs. Barzak leaned forward, a knife in his hand. His arm came down on the first of his victims, Abdoulaye's friend. The latter shifted, and the knife struck the shoulder blade, causing only a flesh wound. Barzak had to make two more attempts, three, till blood spurted up amid the mingled shouts of the victim and the perpetrators. Dramé heard what was going on but couldn't see anything, because the sole of a shoe was pressing on his neck, forcing his face against the floor. The first victim let out a hoarse gasp, his lungs punctured. He was already dying.

"Your turn!" Barzak said, passing the bloody weapon to Slimane Derwich.

Before Slimane knew what was happening, the knife was in his hand. His head spinning, he raised his arm and struck. He was surprised to see the blade sink so easily into Dramé's flesh, gore oozing onto the handle. He let go at once, terrified by his act. He straightened up, his gaze distraught. While the others were kicking furiously at the two bodies, Derwich, his mind in a whirl, watched the scene for several seconds; then his instinct prompted him to get out of the room that second.

He found himself rushing downstairs, taking four steps at a time, followed by all the others. Outside, the air, thick as molasses, stifled him; he ran into the maze of alleyways and only slowed down when his brain seemed to resume control. He walked quickly through the impenetrable night; he felt as if the entire city could hear his footsteps echoing on the paving slabs. He tried to calm down, to gather his thoughts, but it wasn't easy; guilt prevented him from reviewing what had come about a few minutes before in that shabby room. He felt the need to take shelter in his own walls. He avoided the gaze of the shadows he passed. He even had the impression that they were stepping aside as he came by. What he had done must be reflected in his face; anyone could read the infamy written there. Fists clenched, jaw tight, eyes filled with tears, he let out a groan. The scene of carnage he'd just taken part in had utterly overwhelmed him, in its timing and its horror. He rubbed his hands unthinkingly on his pants and looked at them. There was a brownish film between his fingers. He broke into a run again until he was a hundred yards or so from the Café Jdid, where he slowed down, doing his best to wipe the frantic expression off his face.

8

GREENHOUSE EFFECT

ABOUT A WEEK LATER, when Sese passed through the door into the courtyard after taking a walk, he was set upon by the children, who were more excited than usual. They all started talking at once.

"Calm down!" Sese said. He'd heard the word *police* in the hubbub. "What's happened? Mounia, you tell me."

The eldest began to explain: "Some police officers came and took Monsieur Derwich away."

"There were lots of them, in uniform and not," Tawfik said.

"They had so many guns," Bilal added.

"They knocked on the door," Mounia went on. "When Monsieur Derwich opened it and when he saw them, he started crying and held out his hands."

"Like this!" Bilal put his wrists forward and twisted up his face, feigning tears.

"They put handcuffs on him and took him away. That was all," Mounia finished.

"Do any of you know why he was arrested?"

There was another babble of voices.

"I see," said Sese.

"Where did they take him?" asked little Ihssan.

Sese took out his phone at once and tapped in a number.

"Hello. I'd like to speak to the inspector." He said this standing up straight, a charismatic look on his face, feigning a Parisian accent. "Yep, make it snappy."

He glanced at the children to see if his air of importance was working. Indeed it was: they were all gazing at him admiringly, smiles of delight on their faces.

"Yes, Mokhtar. I wanted to talk to you about my neighbor, Monsieur Slimane Derwich. He's an OK guy, you know. I mean, he isn't exactly friendly, but—oh, really? All right."

Sese hung up, looking flummoxed. Mme Bouzid had just come out. She asked, "Did you hear about Derwich?"

"Yes, I'm looking into it. See you later."

And off he went.

Twenty minutes later he was on Rue Goulmima. He passed the arcades, crossed the street, entered the building, and knocked on the third-floor door. When Dramé opened it, his smile at seeing Sese turned into a grimace of pain. He held his wounded stomach with one hand.

"When did you get out of the hospital?"

"This morning. When I called you, I'd just been discharged. How are you, Sese? How are things back home?"

"Don't start with that. Everyone's fine, my uncles, my aunts, Lalah Saïda . . ."

Dramé began to laugh but stopped at once. His wound wouldn't allow it.

"You should sit down."

Dramé sat on one of the mattresses. Three other guys were already there. Each one shook Sese's hand.

"I'm the one who should be asking how you're doing."

"It was real close! See?"

He lifted his T-shirt, revealing a large square dressing.

"Half an inch the other way, and he would have finished me off with that knife of his, I'm telling you, man. God is great. No more swindling for me, Sese. *Wallah!* I'm gonna wait for a commodities market to open up here in Casa and become a trader. It's better; it's more honest. I'm only alive because the blade slipped as it cut through one of my dreads. That was what saved me—look." He showed one of his dreadlocks with a big notch in it. "That cut there is a sign, man. It's like God was personally warning me."

"Yeah, I was just talking with Inspector Daoudi on the phone. They've arrested a suspect, and it's my neighbor. I can't believe it."

"The men that tried to kill me, especially the one who stuck the knife in—I'd recognize him anywhere, even in a hundred years. They were holding me down, but for a second I got a good look at him."

"That's why I wanted to take you along. I don't get it. He's a bookish type, that guy. Though it's also true he's been acting weird the last few days. We've barely seen him, and when he walks by, it's like he was hugging the wall."

"I'll come with you. I want to see the face of the people that killed Abdoulaye's friend. He'd just come to see me; it was pure chance that he was even here, you know."

"I'll go find us a cab. You shouldn't be walking in your condition."

"Whatever you say, man."

At the police station Inspector Daoudi had them brought in almost at once.

"How are you, inspector?" said Sese, shaking hands across the desk.

Dramé did the same.

"How's the wound?" asked Daoudi.

"It's all right; I'm on the mend. They took good care of me at the hospital. But it was close."

"I know, my friend. That's why I've been doing all I can to track down the culprits. We've got one of them; the others are still at large. But we're not through questioning your neighbor. It's true that it's been a tough case; we've had to do a lot of cross-checking and detailed work. But so it goes! God is great."

Daoudi was telling the truth about the inquiry. Derwich's arrest, though, had been disconcertingly easy. It had only needed a few days, during which they gathered all the witness statements, and the job was done. Because everyone had seen him—Derwich—running, distraught, blood on his hands. The alleyways hadn't been as deserted as he thought; the openings in the walls seemed blind, but they weren't. The shadows he'd passed had turned out to be witnesses. Almost a dozen of them had lined up in front of a small peephole to identify the suspect. In addition, aside from the traces of blood on his hands, Slimane Derwich showed the same signs of distress as on the night of the attack. He was unable to say anything about his accomplices, except that the ringleader had been wearing an Olympique de Marseille soccer shirt and a small Gucci cap, with a small bag of the same brand slung across his shoulder—this he swore on his own mother's head. Slimane also remembered that there had been something boyish about him, to the point that Slimane had thought he was harmless.

"You can go check if he's your man," Daoudi said to Dramé, "but it's not worth the effort. All the IDs are positive."

The inspector got up.

"I can't say any more—it's an ongoing investigation, I'm sure you understand. Ask Detective Choukri at the desk to take you down for the identification. Take care."

Sese was on his feet but lingered behind.

"What about Ichrak—do you have any news?"

"It's complicated, that case. We're still looking. But soon, in-shallah," said the inspector with a sigh.

He shook Sese's hand one more time.

Sese was feeling low. He'd messed around the whole day, spent the evening with Cameroonians and Gabonese discussing the relative merits of the Congolese singer Fally Ipupa and the Cameroonian soccer player Samuel Eto'o when it came to fashion and cars. Yet his heart hadn't been in it. He came back home, went into his room, and turned on his computer, but without expecting much. Sure enough, on the screen there was nothing but a string of faces of anonymous women who seemed to have come directly from the beauty parlor. Every one of them announced that she was sensitive, loved the arts and walks in the country, wanted to travel and discover new places.

Sese was beginning to feel truly bored when he heard a call tone with an almost aquatic resonance. He clicked on Accept. The face that appeared on full screen was a familiar one. He turned up the sound and moved his microphone closer to his mouth. He then donned his famous commercial smile—the saintliest guy imaginable—because the lady in question had favored him two or three times with a transfer of a hundred euros. The last one had been several weeks ago. He hadn't heard from her again and thought that she'd dumped him already, like the others, since each time she'd made a big fuss before sending the money.

"How are you?" Sese began. The woman went by the evocative screen name of Sweet Solange. She gave him a long stare. It was no doubt caused by the length of the fiber-optic cable between Morocco and Europe, but Sese was thinking rather that there are some neurons that take more time than others to deliver information to the cortex. He couldn't make out her expression—there was a blueish reflection on her glasses that hid her eyes and prevented a rapid assessment.

"How are you, darling?" he repeated. "Thank you for the Western Union; it was so nice of you."

"That was a while ago! I haven't heard a word since then."

"I had my informatics courses. And I got some bad news from Kinshasa. You remember I told you about my aunt who brought me up? Well, she's had a relapse. I didn't want to bother you with it, so I hesitated to call. I need to find three hundred dollars as soon as possible. The doctors are talking about dialysis. I can't just sit here doing nothing, and I'm so far away from her . . ."

Sese didn't dwell on the unexpected turn the illness had taken. He changed the subject adroitly and looked for a smile to appear on his interlocutor's face. He confided in her concerning his daily struggles as a migrant trapped in Morocco, hoping for the chance to cross the Strait of Gibraltar. Without overdoing it, he spoke of endless lines waiting in the sun for a little food from the Moroccan government. Not pointing any fingers, he told her about having to keep a low profile every day for fear of the constant police checks. But he wasn't complaining, because it would be valuable training for when he'd finally be in France. The truth was that what he most hated, what really brought him down, was the difficulty in his present situation of finding time when the two of them could be alone together, because he was squatting in a two-hundred-square-foot cellar with twelve other African companions, and everyone knows how hard it is to get a good internet connection underground. Especially because they were using the neighbors' Wi-Fi, and those people were constantly downloading stuff. It was a source of great pain to him not to be able to spend more time with the woman he was already deeply in love with. He finally returned to the matter of his family back home and the dialysis treatments, each of which cost more than ten times the monthly salary of a Congolese civil servant. Since his aunt was widowed, it was down to him, whom she regarded as her only son, to come to her aid. Sese began to see not a smile but something much better: a look of sympathy. In other words, the hope of being able to make ends meet till the end of the month.

"Koffi, my sweet?"

That was the name Sese was using. It had a more African ring than Sese Seko, which sounded like it could be Japanese or something. You had to avoid Asian-sounding names; everyone knew that. Asia was not where European women went shopping for sex and love.

"Yes, my little chick?"

Sese had also been thinking about how they adored being called animal names. He was right: the smile of compassion turned into a timid yet flirtatious pout.

"Can I ask you for something, Koffi?"

"Of course!" he murmured, adding a word or two about the "special" affection he felt for her.

"Will you show me your thing?"

"My thing? What do you mean?"

"You know, your thing. What do they call it in that country of yours? Your whatsit."

"Listen, Solange, it's tricky; I don't know if I—"

"You're Koffi the Great Ngando, aren't you? So show me it, that crocodile of yours."

"My little kitten—"

"Do you want your money or not?"

"Yes, but this is an Islamic country. There are some things I can't do."

"You're Muslim?"

"No, not at all, but I stand with them."

"I want proof that you love me. Go on, baby; show me, just a bit. I've never seen a black one."

"Come off it, Solange! It's me, your Koffi!"

"Will you show me or not?"

"Just a second. There's someone at the door; it's the neighbor that has the Wi-Fi. I'll call you back in a minute!"

Sese turned off the camera, pulled off his headset, and rose to his feet. Damn! He was mad at himself for letting things get out of hand. At the beginning of his career as a brouteur, he'd never have stumbled like that. He was unshakable back then. But Solange was right: How could he prove his love if not by presenting, like a certificate, a convincing erection?

"Can you believe her!" Sese swore to himself. "What about my decency? Asking for something like that at a time when all I needed was a little material help, and I wasn't ready yet to leap into virtual sex. What's the big hurry? Can't we talk first? Have a conversation? What's three hundred dollars to her? They're all the same, those women!" he concluded, trying to console himself. He went outside to get some fresh air on his doorstep. Let the moon and stars at least be witnesses to his misfortune.

At some point, he raised his head to the heavens and the Eagle of Kawele.[1]

"Mo Prezo, na baye. Nakomi lokola mwan' etsike, Vié. Ichrak, kaka, Vié na ngai! Mo Prezo, I've had enough! I'm like an orphan, Great Man! There was only Ichrak! Plus, the women are starting to regard me as an adversary. Am I supposed to just pack up shop? And then what? Try to cross to Gibraltar, head for Madrid . . . What does Madrid have that this place doesn't?

---

1. Author's Note: One of the names by which Mobutu was known, along with Great Leopard, Papa Marshal, and the Guide. On a personal note, my first three children, born in Zaire, uttered the name of Mobutu before they knew how to say "papa" or "mama." For one of them it was "Tututu," for the other two, "Papa Bo." (Just before the daily news, Mobutu would appear before a crowd and ask us, "Papa bo? Mama bo? Ekolo bo? Mokonzi bo? How many fathers? How many mothers? How many nations? How many leaders?" The people would respond to each question: "Moko! One!" "Thank you!" he would then say.)

Papers? I feel comfortable here. You chose this country as your final resting place. I think I'm going to do the same. I'll go to Rabat, to the Christian cemetery, throw myself on your grave, and maybe ask for an audience with Mama Bobi Ladawa, your widow, and if she agrees to see me, we'll be able to speak about you for a while. This woman wants to hurt me financially because I'm standing up to her. In your case, when someone stood up to you, if they did it bravely, you'd give them an official post or simply hand over the government. Yet despite your legendary magnanimity, some of them refused. Ingrates. Me, I'm only objecting to the impossible, and all of a sudden I'm looked down on. What kind of democracy is that, eh? You can't even call it a 'process.' Also, when it comes to solidarity with the Arab world, it was you who taught me everything. Did you not say, on October 4, 1973, at the UN General Assembly: 'Between a friend and a brother, the choice is clear: I choose the brother'? And you broke off diplomatic relations with Israel because they'd gone too far in annexing Egyptian territory. Many African countries followed suit. And me, what am I doing today? Should I not follow you? When I'm your *pur petit*—your true little brother? You see how they are, Great Man. Like the international community. You want to remain true to yourself? All of a sudden, they become pitiless, cut off your money, freeze your assets, stir up a revolt against you in the North or in the East. If you're an Arab? They fabricate a false spring like the ones with the jihadists, who start by killing Muslims, with a total lack of bismillah—mercy. They're diabolical."

It wasn't late, but the courtyard had emptied of the children, who brought life to it from morning to evening whenever they weren't at school. Such moments reminded Sese of just how isolated he was in this foreign country. Ichrak was gone, and a part of his new life had departed with her. At her side, a disaster like the one he'd just had would never have happened. Everything was so much easier when she was around. At the least feeling of stress, her laughter rising in the air, like the singing of angels, made you forget even the existence of death. And things didn't always go smoothly in their line of work. For instance, there were certain menacing remarks that "clients" had made. There were dissatisfied customers who perhaps lived in this country, maybe even in Casablanca itself. It had happened that Sese followed through on his threat to reveal everything to family and friends, when he'd been able to track them down online. The world was small, and their prey had seen Ichrak's face as well as her cleavage. Sese only hoped that one of them had not met his friend on that tragic night. He'd begun to realize that certain things needed to be thought through before they were put into action, even if, in his mind, his blackmailing activities were purely a matter of payback for online perverts.

The day of Ichrak's death, Sese had gone to see her very early in the morning, and he'd come upon the crowd gathered around her body. She'd called him late the previous evening, distraught: her mother was in a bad way; she needed money. Sese had promised to give her some the next morning. He was expecting a transfer; he would swing by and pick her up in Derb Taliane so they could go together as soon as the Western Union office opened. She must have gone out in the middle of the night to the pharmacist she knew in hopes of getting the medication on credit, and in that way she had met her fate.

As for the police, Daoudi didn't seem to have any leads yet regarding who might have done it. No suspect had emerged. At this point, anyone could have killed her. It was true that Ichrak's unruly character got under many people's skin, but from there to murdering her . . . Strangely, the inspector didn't seem to be putting much effort into the case. He gave nothing but vague answers to Sese's questions. Too vague, to Sese's mind, given that like everyone else, he'd known the victim well. As he thought about this lack of interest, the young Congolese began to ask himself how well Ichrak and Daoudi had actually known one another. He only knew one thing about their relationship: "He's a swine; he's worse than a dog!" That was how Ichrak had spoken of the inspector. She hated him, and her contempt for him was even stronger than her hatred. He had arrested her one evening, and something must have happened in the cell where she'd briefly been held. You don't call a cop a swine just because he arrests you. There was definitely some secret between them. Daoudi was unscrupulous, true, but was he actually capable of eliminating a girl like Ichrak? To keep her from talking? About what? Out of pride? Maybe. Mokhtar wasn't beyond getting rid of someone for some major business dealing, but a woman like Ichrak could only have been murdered for reasons of passion, as claimed by certain lawyers who know nothing about love. In Sese's view, Daoudi didn't match the profile of a crazed lover.

From opposite, a voice diverted his thoughts. He heard a particularly high-pitched volley of words issuing from the impressive throat of Lalah Saïda. The door opened, and the cause of this outburst—Ihssan, as it turned out—trotted calmly across to Sese and stopped in front of him.

"Where's my present?"

"I haven't forgotten you, sweetie; it's just that I was late getting home."

Sese reached into his pocket and produced a candy. "Here, honey, enjoy it."

"Thank you."

Ihssan held the gift in both hands, not unwrapping it at once. She stared at it and turned it slowly in her fingers. Then she looked up and asked, "Are you sad because your friend has gone?"

"Yes, Ihssan. But that's life; I have to manage. Eat your candy; don't worry about me."

"Ihssan, come back here!"

Mme Saïda had just appeared. She was standing in the doorway, hands on hips, hair disheveled.

"Ihssan, stop bothering Sese. Come and eat your supper! You should come too, Sese. How are you, actually?"

"I already ate, Lalah Saïda."

"All alone in your corner like the last few days? It's as if you've not eaten at all. You'll end up losing weight if you're not careful. Come eat with us."

"Thank you, big sister, but I'm fine."

"I'll have Mounia bring you something over, in case you get hungry later on. You never know. And you—come here, Ihssan. Run away again instead of sitting down to eat and you'll see what I'll do to you."

The little girl ran back. Not because she was frightened by the threat but to let her mother hold on to her illusions about the extent of her natural authority.

Exposed to the gusts of Chergui whipping at his face, Sese had had enough of contemplating the stars. He went back inside. He hadn't left the mosquitoes of Kinshasa to their fate just to be landed with this sort of nighttime nuisance. Sitting in front of his computer, he thought about his future. Since the death of his friend, he really had thought of himself as an orphan. Continuing on northward and trying to settle yet again did not appeal to him in the least. Here there was the Bouzid family, his friends, his familiar places, the country that was developing at high speed. For some time, he'd been thinking of going to see Zahira and introducing himself. As an African he was embarrassed not to have done so sooner, not to have offered his support in her grief. In any case, he ought to go to her. He had no choice—he was the only one, aside from Ichrak, who was familiar with all the symptoms of her illness and also one of the few who knew about her medication and where it could be obtained.

His conversation with Sweet Solange had made him think too. Before he met Ichrak, an idea had been hounding him. He'd driven it away, but it kept coming back. At that time, feeling a little desperate, he'd thought that if he asked one of his lady friends to come to Morocco, for a vacation for instance, he could easily have convinced her to marry him at city hall. That way, if he played his cards right, he could get himself a Schengen visa and rejoin her later, calmly, following legal procedures. Since he'd never found the time to learn to swim, in order to avoid the challenge of the sea, he'd found this a pragmatic, compromise solution. Solange had always played him hard, but—Sese sensed it—she couldn't live without him, and she'd do anything to ensure his company. With her there could be possibilities. Since then Sese had changed, and as he thought back, he got goose bumps. From now on, there was no longer any question of straying into marriage or of preparing himself mentally for administrative coitus. He planned to set in motion the necessary procedures and quite simply legalize his situation. It was at this point in his thoughts that a call signal trilled, and Sweet Solange's name flashed up on the screen as if Sese's cogitations had summoned up a trial. He slipped on his headset, adopted a relaxed pose, assumed a half-smile, broadened it into a grin, and clicked on the icon bearing the almost psychoanalytic word *accept*. Solange's spectacles appeared at once, along with a sound as if she were bursting out of a bubble.

"My little kitten!" he said, in his best butter-wouldn't-melt voice.

9

HIGH PRESSURE

DAOUDI WAS SQUATTING ON THE SIDEWALK, in the exact spot where Ichrak's body had been found. He passed a finger over the ground and took a long look at the dust it picked up, as if it might give him a lead—a clue as to how to proceed. He looked around. Nothing connects with anything else, he griped to himself. How can a report be put together in these conditions? Not many people were about. Nothing was moving. What could be felt was the presence of Chergui, sweeping through the bowels of these alleyways like a Rolls-Royce Series 1000 jet engine. A further drop of pressure since early that morning had made the air even more unpredictable than before. A gust of wind from who knew where blew up and swirled around the inspector; he felt his suit sticking to him and vibrating like a pneumatic drill. The tails of his jacket and the cuffs of his pants flapped like ISIS banners. He was forced to turn aside by the hail of sand that followed, striking his face in an open-handed slap. Before any counterattack came, there was a brief moment of calm beneath the dazzling sun.

It was a vicious killing, but Daoudi couldn't think what the motive could be. Ichrak came from a modest background and had mostly led an uneventful life. In such a case, how could the slit throat be explained? Rue du Poète Taha Adnan was quiet. The passersby and the ironmongers in their shops were going about their business as usual. As was the sun. It reflected off the walls painted acrylic white and flooded the area with a harsh light. The inspector, narrowing his eyes and still squatting, wondered how he was going to close the case. He'd long since read the report from the forensic institute, which had not provided any significant information. The wound had been caused by a sharp instrument, probably a blade, which had not entered deeply but had proved fatal: the carotid artery had been severed clean through. Apart from this cut and the marks from the victim's fall down the steps, there were no other injuries.

Daoudi took out his phone to look at the photos he'd taken a few weeks ago. He flipped through them and found the ones he was looking for. He went back up the steps to the street at the top, then moved fifty yards or so to the left. Checking on one of the pictures, he found the place where the traces of blood had begun. The image showed them, spread over a small area. Had the victim tried to get away from her attacker by fighting back? Definitely not—he would have struck her again, and there was no sign of such a thing. Or else, after being cut she spun around in place, hence the spatter. Daoudi tried to connect the parts, like editing a film. Retracing his steps, eyes on his phone screen, he stopped halfway, where there was another concentration of brown marks.

Had the victim made a pause, so to speak, at this spot? It was strange to think of Ichrak as "the victim," yet she was, even though Daoudi couldn't get her out of his mind. He let out a groan to give vent to his morbid thoughts. He moved forward some more, went back down the steps, and returned to where the body had been found at dawn: the place where the young woman had fallen, unconscious, and had bled to death.

"Why does death arrive in such a simple way?" Mokhtar Daoudi asked himself. He believed firmly in the concept of *maktoob*, or destiny, but the speed at which the young woman had gone from being alive to being dead left him with a bitter taste, like those times where you're certain something will never be brought to a close, whatever you might do. In this case, the inspector was experiencing contradictory feelings that still took him by surprise. In dying, she had deprived him of the chance to take his revenge for the worst humiliation he'd ever experienced at the hands of a woman. Daoudi still couldn't forgive himself for his weakness that day, in the cell, when he'd spilled his seed, out of fear, like a coward, on Ichrak's thighs, failing to take from her that which he had desired so intensely. He had wanted to have her in his grip, yet he had fallen into hers. After that incident, he'd had to withstand her scornful gaze whenever they passed in the street or, worse, be met with her indifference when she walked by, her own woman, feigning not to notice him. A dog would not have known such degradation. Her insolence was boundless. Who would not have wanted to force her to lower her eyes? Every time, the wound she inflicted was like a red-hot iron applied to his soul. To overcome this feeling, he would have needed to force himself on her the way a man should. Now that she was dead, Ichrak left him to his suffering. Mokhtar Daoudi had hoped for a while that the shame perpetually dwelling in him would finally abate, but so far that had not happened.

On one of the photos, his attention was drawn to a detail aside from the brown marks. He returned up the steps and along the street and stopped in front of a utility pole bearing a poster for a soccer game—the Casablanca match between Wydad FC and Raja CA. The pole also held up, or had held up, a metal cable—probably a phone line. The pole had shifted on its cement pedestal and was leaning at perhaps thirty degrees; given the narrowness of the road, it had probably been struck at some time by a vehicle. Daoudi took hold of it and moved it with one hand; it turned like crazy. The cable trailed across the ground along the roadway. Putting away his phone, Daoudi picked up the copper wire at the place where it had snapped. He examined it along three feet or so of its length. Around him, scraps of paper and dry leaves were shifting sluggishly about in a new eddy less forceful than the last. This one wasn't disorienting. Quite the opposite, it helped the inspector to think; it inspired him, even. He pulled the cable to one side and slid it between his fingers till he reached its end. He held it for another moment like this, then let it go with a sigh.

"If the death of that young woman isn't a pure expression of maktoob, I, Mokhtar Daoudi, cannot see how it could be anything else, I swear. And when maktoob steps in, it's best to keep clear of the waves."

Saying this to himself, he headed unhurriedly toward the Dacia that was parked close by.

For two or three days, the atmospheric pressure had risen from 1,013 or so to the exceptional level of 1,054 hectopascals in Casa, which gave many the impression that Chergui had lowered in intensity. In fact, Daoudi took it as a wish for an alliance. Something that could wipe away the last traces of dunes and oases in the Sahara would know how to get rid of memories that were flaying the hearts of human beings. Mokhtar Daoudi couldn't get over the incident with Ichrak in the cell. Above all because, despite the bedazzlement that had driven him toward realizing his desire, a stubborn latent shame lingered in his mind: he'd disappointed himself. He had imagined possessing the young woman, but when he thought he was about to do it, nothing in the world could hold back the come that had spurted from him or the long moan he uttered at the very moment he was brushing against the lips of paradise. Daoudi would never forget the way the woman recoiled and her disdainful grimace as the lower part of his body, slumped against her, emptied itself in spasms. She detached herself from the mass pressing down on her, rose from the bunk of the jail cell where the act had taken place, and lowered her dress, which he had lifted to the level of her hips. She picked up her leather clutch, knocked to the floor a short time before, opened it, and took out a Kleenex. She unhurriedly wiped the inside of her thigh and examined the result. She then straightened her clothing, looking Mokhtar Daoudi scornfully up and down as she did so, and threw the Kleenex to him.

"You didn't take anything from me. Check it out. It's all there."

Daoudi averted his gaze.

"Take a good look, don't be afraid. You're like a dog. Though even a dog wouldn't have done what you just did. You can keep those," she added, pointing to the crumpled piece of white lace that the cop had torn off and tossed on the ground. "You're pathetic, Mokhtar; you tore them for no reason."

Her expression unruffled, she moved toward the door, which Daoudi had not had the presence of mind to lock. Sitting dazedly on the bunk, he knew as well as she did that he had gotten nothing out of it except that sticky wad of tissue: a little pool of cold sperm wiped from the top of her thigh. His pleasure had overcome him and sunk him before he could even take her, however eagerly he had wanted to do so.

～

Sitting in Mokhtar Daoudi's office, Zahira watched the inspector's mouth formulating the outcome of the inquiry into her daughter's death. But she no longer heard anything. Her brain was in turmoil. She was asking herself why this man kept talking even though no sound came out. When she became aware of the peculiar silence, her hearing seemed to return. A sound like a rumbling in the belly was informing her that after a difficult investigation, the facts that had emerged suggested that the incident had been a matter of chance: Ichrak had been in the wrong place at the wrong time; it was an unfortunate accident. In the first part of his speech, the inspector had mentioned a sandstorm, a game between Raja and Wydad, a wobbly pole, something about a broken cable, and a whip that cuts young women's throats by night. Everything was topsy-turvy in Zahira's mind.

"You just have to accept it, *Hajja*. Accidents happen all the time. Sign here."

"Accept?" Zahira said, bridling. "Accept what?"

The repetition of the word *accident* was more than she could endure. She leaped to her feet in the fullness of her body and began screaming: "You killed Ichrak! You killed my Ichrak! But look at me—I'm not completely dead. Finish me off if you have the guts. Coward! You're cowards, the lot of you! Finish me! What are you waiting for?"

Truly raving now, Zahira began to tear at her clothing as she barked curses upon Daoudi and all the men who inhabited the earth and upon the fathers, brothers, uncles who had betrayed her and been unable to defend her. The inspector was utterly overwhelmed. He was on his feet too, shouting for his men to come and take away this crazy woman. The door opened, and four officers dashed in, Choukri among them.

"Do you always go around in fours? Finish me off! Twenty-nine years! Twenty-nine years and I'm still here! You killed my daughter! She was given her name to wipe away that night. Ichrak was my only light, and you've taken her away from me." She was weeping like a child. The police officers took hold of Zahira any way they could. Her size and her fury made it very difficult. Choukri's cap tumbled to the floor. Zahira struggled, trying to throw herself to the ground. To get her out of the office, they virtually had to carry her, like a dead weight, or rather like a dying body whose limbs were still thrashing.

"Kill me!" she was shouting. "Kill me like the oud player did that night. Oud player, I curse you! A curse upon you!"

Then she began to sing:

La ana addi esh-shuq
Wi layali esh-shuq
Wa la albi addi azabu, azabu
Tol omri ba'ul.

As she kept on tearing her clothes and wrestling to free herself from the grip of the men, Zahira was singing the words of "Seret El Hob," Umm Kulthum's ode to love, which had moved her so back then and led to her grave being dug in a courtyard near Bab Marrakech. Since then, that grave had been awaiting its body, so far in vain. Daoudi, on the other hand, was no longer shouting. The words coming from Zahira's mouth had made him sit back down at his desk, thunderstruck, and had forced him to think. In particular about the secret surrounding the birth of Ichrak, the identity of the man who'd gotten her mother pregnant, who had put his seed in her. During the tussle, Daoudi had heard what the woman was yelling; he also caught sight of an indigo tattoo of a moon and two crescents on the curve of her shoulder. The memory of his mouth fastening on something blue and the quivering flesh of an unknown woman came flooding back to him.

Now that the tumult in the room was over, Daoudi found himself facing that young officer who, twenty-nine years earlier, had played the oud so well and whose abilities drew beautiful women, like a powerful talisman, to the guardhouse of a municipal building. "I curse you, oud player!" still sounded from the next room, like a judicial sentence. Mokhtar Daoudi had believed naively that the agonizing sensation of red-hot irons on his soul was his final ordeal. He was now aware that the flames, as if fanned by djinns, had already begun to take hold of him but that they would never totally consume him—of this he was certain—and so it would go on for all eternity. Chergui had accorded him only a small favor in giving him the illusion of an alliance. His pride had made him think of a privilege like an endless cord, like the jars of paradise that can never be emptied. Eternity belongs to death; it belongs to the desert wind. How could such an entity make a pact with someone who was less than a dog? Daoudi interrupted his thoughts for a moment, because he was facing a huge battle: the djinns that were stirring the flames in his chest forced him to make extraordinary efforts to suppress the howl rising from his throat like a torrent of fire, and it hurt so much he wanted to rip out his own throat. Since he couldn't do that, he wished that the cry would at least suffocate him entirely, so it would be over, so it would stop.

～

After the events in Casablanca, the atmospheric pressure dropped from 1,054 to around 1,013 over the city, and the air mass resumed its former state. Chergui now had every chance of undertaking a decisive action to lead to some movement. It had lingered over the city only too long. The inhabitants, already sorely tried, could not hold out much more, and no one knew what might happen next. There'd been a huge surge in the number of women struck by hysteria in the Bourgogne, Aïn Chock, and Sbata neighborhoods. The numbers of men who'd gone crazy had beaten all records everywhere, especially in Mohammedia and Sidi Moumen. Despite these alarming facts, it was still the neighborhood of Derb Taliane that had paid the highest price since the time the wind from the Sahara had been trapped and obliged to spin above the town. After the tragic deaths of Ichrak and of Abdoulaye's friend, what else might lie ahead?

Over the Atlantic and in the stratosphere, the forces led by Climate Change and the Gulf Stream had weakened since Chergui and its southern allies had joined up to the east of the Azores High. These allies unleashed attacks aimed at shifting the region of low pressure that was stuck over Casa and pushing it off toward the Mediterranean to create an indraft sufficient for Chergui to use as a trampoline, allowing it to cross the Strait of Gibraltar. The mother of all battles was under way. In the meantime, the Benguela Current had come from the south and was keeping up its ruthless offensive along the coast of Africa, backed by the southeast trades. Because of the deadly hurricanes ravaging the United States, Climate Change had lost much of its power in the eastern Atlantic, being constrained by Chergui and its allies to concentrate exclusively on Texas, Florida, and New Orleans. The Gulf Stream, hemmed in by the Angola, North Equatorial, and Canary Currents, had to continue on its route and also head toward the US, thus intensifying the devastation there tenfold. At this point, Chergui took the risk of sacrificing the population of Casa under a heat wave approaching 110°F. To bring about low pressure over the Mediterranean, an abrupt rise in atmospheric pressure over the city had to be prioritized. The efforts of the southeast trades were far from sufficient; the winds of the region were called in—the Bech, the Levanter, and the Vendavel—and these banded together to provide Chergui with a kind of flying carpet, so it could finally head toward Gibraltar and the Mediterranean shores and, in the guise of the Sirocco, accomplish its destiny, which consisted of sweeping the Balearic Islands, Languedoc, Corsica, Sicily, Sardinia, all the way to the territory of Greece.

Casa was recovering from the disruptions of recent days, but in Derb Taliane the shadow of Ichrak was ever present. In Cuba her memory was still alive; it burned in the flesh on Rue Souss, overran minds on Boulevard Sour Jdid. In this way eternity was expressing itself, and the metallic voice of the muezzin, carried on the winds blowing from the Atlantic, reminded everyone that infinity belongs neither to dogs nor to humans but is the exclusive privilege of souls. Who would dare deny that? Nobody. In any case, no one in the city of Casablanca, also known as Ad-dar Al Baidaa'.

In Koli Jean Bofane was born in 1954 in the northern region of what is today the Democratic Republic of Congo; he currently resides in Belgium. His novels have received numerous awards, including the Grand Prix littéraire de l'Afrique noire, the Grand Prix du Roman Métis, and the Prix des Cinq continents de la Francophonie. He is the author of *Congo, Inc.* (Indiana University Press, 2018).

Bill Johnston's awards include the PEN Translation Prize, the Best Translated Book Award, and the National Translation Award in Poetry. He teaches literary translation at Indiana University Bloomington.